Dream Lover and Other Tales

Dream Lover
and
Other Tales

RjCook

Copyright (C) 2016 RjCook
Layout design and Copyright (C) 2016 Creativia
Published 2016 by Creativia
Book design by Creativia (www.creativia.org)
Cover art by http://www.thecovercollection.com/
This book is a work of fiction. Names, characters, places, and incidents are the product of the author's imagination or are used fictitiously. Any resemblance to actual events, locales, or persons, living or dead, is purely coincidental.
All rights reserved. No part of this book may be reproduced or transmitted in any form or by any means, electronic or mechanical, including photocopying, recording, or by any information storage and retrieval system, without the author's permission.

Contents

Glint	1
Dream Lover	15
Ben Franklin's Dream	54
The Mayor's Cow	59
The Maestro's Gift	64
Tracks in the Snow	90
The Messiah of Harriman	95
About the Author	142

Glint

I can't get my mind to stop, can't get my thoughts to shut up even for a moment. Seems I'm in a cranial war with myself, battling the depression that is trying so earnestly to get over the wall I've built inside. When you've fought as long and as hard as I have there is no considering surrendering. It's all or nothing. If and when I lose it, it will be total, complete.

I reach into my backpack for the hooded sweatshirt I'm now happy I decided to take with me. It fits snuggly over the two pullover tees and long-sleeved button work shirt I'm wearing, along with a pair of blue sweatpants over my brown cargo shorts. The Nevada desert is cold at night, not a place to sleep of my choosing but this is where my ride dropped me off. "Tempest" he called himself, not sure if that was his name or just a label he grew up with. Picked me up back in California, just outside of Berkeley, said he had a place in San Francisco and was going to visit his son who lived with his ex somewhere in southern Nevada. Wasn't really interested in his life story but a ride is a ride.

Hitch-hiking really sucks, you know? People think it's dangerous, or its romantic and mysterious, the life of the wanderer, the road warrior traveling from and to points unknown. Bullshit. It's mostly boring, standing on the side of a road for hours on end, being hassled by cops or assholes in cars who get a thrill by chucking soda cans or whatever at you as they race by. But unfortunately sometimes it's necessary. Like now, for me. I need to get back east, to Jersey, and I don't have much money and there is no one to turn to for help.

California living was a bust, living in a flea bag motel, unable to find a decent job, and then some shit came down that made me pack up what I could carry and head east. A sleeping bag, three shirts, a hoodie, pair of shorts and sweatpants, a small hand towel with a map of the State of New Jersey imprinted on it, an empty cloth bag, "Speed", a paperback novel by William Burroughs, and my Italian Stiletto switchblade I took as payment for a few ounces of weed I was helping some dude unload. He didn't want it, said they were illegal. Funny, I thought, the guy is selling weed here in Berkeley, 1974, and he is worried about carrying an illegal blade. Sucker is sharp, though, and it snaps out quicker than you can blink. Guess it's good to have here on the road. You never know. I used it to cut up an apple Tempest gave me.

Anyway, it's cold and dark now. I've found a place to settle down for the night, on the outskirts of a small town. I've spread out my sleeping bag atop a low hill, or sand dune, away from the road. I won't be visible to anyone driving by till the sun comes up, but I'll probably be awake by then. I rarely sleep well on the road.

Sure enough, the next morning I'm up with the sun, the last nighttime star fading in the west. I pack up my things and head into the nearby town. I've decided to live mostly on coffee and buttered rolls on my journey, that will stretch my money out if I can make any decent time getting rides. There is a diner in the middle of town, an old place on the ground floor of an even older hotel. Reminds me of a western saloon I've seen in the movies. It's got a long counter with a line of stools next to it, tables spread out in no particular pattern on the floor. Overhead there are several large wooden fans turning slowly, hanging from a high, tin ceiling.

It's not crowded when I walk in but everyone who is here stops what they're doing and looks up. The place becomes gripped in a ghostly silence. I know I look like a real mess and smell even worse, so can't say I blame them. The guy behind the counter takes my order, hands me my coffee and roll in a paperbag even though I didn't say it was to go. It was, and I turn and leave without looking up. Maybe I should be grateful it's not the wild west any longer, no one coming up to me and saying "we don't cater to your kind in this here town" and pulling me into a gunfight out in the street.

The Nevada sun heats up the day early. I strip down to shorts and a tee shirt, walk to the eastern end of town and find a good spot on the highway to put my thumb out. My first and only ride of the day is a woman named Kathy, middle-aged, and I'm guessing older in appearance than her years. Gives me the impression she was a looker in her younger years but heavy smoking has taken its toll. She has a lit cigarette in her mouth and the car reeks of burnt tobacco.

"Where you headin', hun?" she asks.

"As far east as you can take me" I reply.

"Well then, hop in." Kathy says, " looks like we'll be keepin' each other company for a bit."

Kathy is nice, but as with most rides the obligatory dissemination of our lives begins. I don't reveal too much of myself to strangers, and a lot of what I do say is made up. I figure might as well embellish my existence in exciting past endeavors: residing in exotic locales, growing up in a large family or alone since I was very young, raised on a farm or in a big city, or in a commune, roadied for Hendrix...I've done it all when relaying my fictional life to that point in time to those kind enough to give me a ride. Kathy's story is straight forward. She's heading to a new job, husband died in Vietnam, no kids. Seems she's got a degree in animal husbandry and an offer from some children's zoo in Nashville. I'm guessing it's not a lucrative career, judging by what she drives and the boxes in the back seat that represent her life. The dashboard has a plastic Jesus on it, right hand up blessing all those cars behind us.

I enjoy my time with Kathy and the day goes by quickly. She gets me as far as a truck stop somewhere in Colorado before she heads south to New Mexico to visit a friend. I thank her for the ride, wish her the best of luck in her new job and head into the truck stop's diner. Haven't eaten since early in the morning so I grab a booth and treat myself to their meatloaf special which looks terrible but really wasn't so bad.

When I'm on the road and in a diner or store, I keep my eyes down. No interest in making eye contact with anyone who might want to start a conversation, asking what it's like living like I do, where are you heading, etc. But this time I can't help but notice the two men at the counter watching me, exchanging whispers, stealing furtive glances my way. A black guy and a white guy, maybe in their forties, and for sure they're truck drivers. Stout, stocky, the white guy is heavier, wearing suspenders over his flannel shirt, the black guy is in good shape, wearing a pullover shirt that reads AB MOVERS across the chest. All I can do is ignore them, finish my meal, pay the check and leave. But ignoring them isn't going to work, they follow me outside. It's dark by this time, the parking lot lights are on, there are a few cars parked near the diner.

"Boy" the white guy yells, "wait up, boy." I turn to meet them, removing my backpack, holding it in front of me. They come too close for comfort.

"You wanna buy some reefer?" the black guy asks.

"No thanks, guys. I'm good" and turn to walk away. I think it's best I stay in the lights.

"Don't walk away from us, son." the white guy bellows. "We want to see what you got in that there bag of yours."

I know I'm in trouble and can see them slowly separating with the intention of one getting behind me. I notice to my left two parked cars with a parking lot light pole between them. Slowly I back between the cars, hoping not to be flanked.

"Look guys, I'm sure you can find a better target to roll. Do I look like I own much of anything?" I plead. Quicker than I anticipated the white guy is upon me.

"Shut your damn mouth, faggot!" he yells and with both hands knocks me to the ground. I'm able to hold onto my backpack but the black guy runs over and attempts to tear it from my grasp. In desperation I reach into the pack for my Stiletto, flick it open and swipe at his shins, cutting through his jeans and slicing open a large gash on his leg. He let's out a blood curdling scream, the white guy backs up in shock and before either can recoup from my defense a few men come storming out of the diner, one screaming "Hey, get away from him." The two who attacked me take off, the black guy limping, practically dragging his leg behind him and my would-be rescuers choose wisely not to persue them. I close the Stiletto and hide it behind the light pole where it's dark in shadow. The men from the diner never saw it. They help me to my feet and walk me back inside, seating me in a booth near the door.

"We called the police", one of them said while a waitress brought me a glass of water.

"Great. Thank you" I reply, but it wasn't great. When you're hitch-hiking across the country the less contact you have with the law, the better. And there was my situation back in California...

Two Colorado state troopers show up. Typical, beefy, ex-military types. One sits in the booth opposite me, the name plate on his shirt reads "Connor", while the other officer leans against the lunch counter. I can't make out the name on his tag. They take my report and description of the two who attacked me.

"Do you require medical assistance" Officer Connor asks.

"No, I'm fine, really."

"Why do you think they attacked you? What's in the bag they could have wanted?"

"No idea," I answer, "I don't have much", but I know where this is heading.

"So you wouldn't mind if we take a look?" the officer leaning against the counter asks.

I was the victim a moment ago, now I'm a suspect. I've been to this dance before.

"If I say no it's going to happen anyway" I answer. The seated cop flashes a shit-eating grin and begins to empty my backpack on the table.

"Is this all you're carrying?" he asks, "Where are you heading?"

"Back home to New Jersey. I'll be on a bus tomorrow". I know enough to not mention I'm bumming for rides, not sure if it's legal here in Colorado.

"I would have guessed Jersey by this" Connor says as he holds up my small hand towel for his partner to see.

"Never been to New Jersey" partner states, "don't think I'd ever want to from what I hear."

I keep my mouth shut, not about to proclaim the high points of my home state to these two rednecks. Nothing much to sell anyway and I'm not a martyr. They tell me I can call their headquarters for a copy of the report in a few days and leave. The waitress brings me a cup of coffee, "on the house" she says, "boss told me to tell you, take your time. Rest as long as you need to."

She is pretty. I thank her and tell her so, I get a wink back and she moves onto the next table. After an hour or so I figure it's time to leave, certain I'm wearing out my welcome and a wink from the pretty waitress is the best I'm going to do. My knife is still where I left it, behind the light pole. I stuff it into my backpack and look for a place to sleep for what's left of the night. Before passing beyond the parked cars I catch a glimpse of myself in a car window, shocked at how thin I've gotten, and forgot that I both cut my long hair short and shaved my beard before leaving California. There's a few days of growth on my face, all the more adding to this straggly look I'm now sporting.

The rest stop has a picnic area where the trucks are parked. I find a picnic table farthest from the parking lot and spread out my sleeping bag beneath it. The night is chilly again and it looks like rain, so I put on every piece of clothing I'm carrying. Before I fall asleep the bad memory of California comes back. I can once again see the clown who let himself into my studio apartment at one in the morning. Recognized him as belonging to the motel's maintenance crew, obviously drunk and obviously not expecting me to be there.

"I, uh…I heard your AC's not working right. Uh…figured I'd check it out" he mumbles, nearly incoherently. He bends to look at my AC which is built low into the wall by my door. I find myself shaking off the cobwebs of deep sleep and quickly find I am flushed with anger, there is a rage inside of me I've never experienced before. This bastard came to rob me, take what was mine. Next to my bed I keep a short iron bar on the advice of my neighbor who told me she's had to use hers in the past.

"SONOFABITCH!" I scream and slam the bar into the side of his head. The force of the blow throws him sideways and he slams his chin on the kitchenette counter. He falls to the floor motionless. "Shit", is all I can think to say, and remain still, listening for any response to the noise from my neighbors or from anyone who might be outside on the walkway.

Nothing. All is calm. There is no blood, but I've put a large indentation on the right side of his skull. There is no pulse in his neck and I can see he's not breathing. What to do? Call the cops? No way they're going to believe he just walked in on me in the middle of the night, and it's obvious I hit him from behind. I do the only thing I can think of: drag him into the bathroom and dump him into the tub. After a few dozen stealth-like trips to the ice machine in the laundry room he is completely covered in ice. Then it's a matter of getting myself out of there. I cut my hair and shave my beard, decide to leave as soon as possible. The roach motel I lived in didn't even bother to ask for i.d. when I took the room and I paid in cash. Sold my van more than a week ago for food money so there's nothing they have to go on when the body is found. I guessed that wouldn't be for awhile. While it was still dark I walk out to 415, that's where Tempest picked me up, and here I am sleeping beneath this old, wooden picnic table somewhere in Colorado. Life can be a bitch.

The morning sun comes too soon. Dreary, and needing a bathroom I walk back to the truck stop diner. It's a different crew working there, they don't recognize me as the guy who was attacked in the parking lot last night but I'm betting they heard the story. I grab a coffee and buttered roll - thinking I'd like to say goodbye to the cute waitress from last evening but can't now - and head to the highway for my next ride.

For most of the day I've got my thumb out and no luck, daylight is slipping away. I walk a bit down the highway, stop each time I see a vehicle approaching, hoping for the best. I'm thinking this day is going to be a bust, I'm about to give up when just before night fall a pickup truck with two young ladies in it pulls over. They tell me they can give me a ride if I'm willing to ride in the open back. No problem I tell them and climb aboard. They've got some soft luggage strapped down and it makes for a nice pillow. The sun sets slowly in the west behind us, the stars overhead one-by-one become more visible until the night sky is a dazzling display of light. There is one particular formation I focus on: it's a grouping of four stars in the shape of a kite. Always intended to learn what constellation they were part of but never got around to it. They are a bitter part of my life, nonetheless.

The night my mother died, after having suffered in bed for ten years as the result of a stroke, I left her bedside not wanting to be there for her last breath. My sisters and father stood by her, holding her hand while I went outside. The first thing I noticed were these same four stars overhead, it was an unusually clear night sky for New Jersey, and I angrily cursed God for all that was happening. Mom and dad lived with me, my sisters' homes were a distance away. All I could think of was now it was just dad and me and that just wouldn't work. We had no use for each other, always at odds ends over every little thing and now with mom gone and he in his later years, it was expected I would take care of him. So it came as a shock to all of them when I announced I was moving west, to California within a week. I know it made my sisters angry and there was a look of worry in my father's eyes, but no way was I getting stuck with him. I packed up my Dodge van and took what few things I had and left.

While it was still dark the girls pulled off the highway into a clearing next to a lake. They said they needed some sleep, I stayed in the back of the truck where, until the light of the next morning I slept deeply and soundly. Shortly after the sun came up I woke to the girls packing up their sleeping bags, getting ready for the road again. They shared a thermos of orange juice, got me as far as the next exit on the highway where they dropped me off, then they drove north. Once again I was in the middle of nowhere, some place in Nebraska. It was starting to feel as if I'd never get home, no one was expecting me so there was no time-table, and I hadn't thought about where I was going to live when I got back to New Jersey. My father had moved in with one of my sisters and I could only assume they were still angry that I left. It would be no welcoming home the prodigal son, all I could do was worry about it when the time came.

But this morning it looked like my luck was changing. While it was still early, the first car that came upon me stopped. This is going well, I thought, until I got into the now-waiting car. He called himself Butch, drove a rundown dark blue 1964 Rambler. He was a stocky man with a gut that hung over the chain belt strung through the loops of his cuffed blue jeans, black tee shirt too tight for his girth, and black working boots on his feet. Butch had tattoos on both arms, one of them a Marine insignia. His face was shaven, hair short, black and spiked with grease that made it stand straight up. The ashtray in the car was overflowing with cigarette butts and it was all I could do to not gag from the odor. He never asked where I was heading, just started driving, and I quickly became uncomfortable with the piercing stares he shared between me and the road.

After a passing of uncomfortable silence I tried to start a conversation - some remark about the weather, or how there was so little to see here in Nebraska - but Butch just grunted with each remark so I gave up. Further down the highway, after maybe a half-hour of driving, he said he needed to make a call. There was a phone booth at the bottom of the next exit that accessed a one-lane road that ran parallel to the highway. That he knew there was a phonebooth there I found disturbing. I sat in the car and I could see him watching me as he spoke into the phone, giving me the distinct impression it was me he was talking about. Butch returned to the car, he was now sweating, seemed anxious. When he began driving I could see he was avoiding the highway. My instincts kicked in and I reached into the backpack that was on my lap and grabbed hold of my Stiletto. We drove for another five minutes when he suddenly turned down a gravel road that had a wired fence on his side with a line of trees behind it. My side there was a short drop to a small creek that ran alongside the road.

"Wait" I said, "where are we going? I don't want any trouble." I was sure he could hear what he thought was fear in my voice but I knew the burning cauldron of anger that was growing inside of me. He grabbed my left thigh with his right hand and squeezed.

"Now boy," he uttered, "we're going to have us some fun. Then I'll drive you to where…"

Without thinking I clicked open my switchblade and with my right hand sliced across the top of his hand on my leg. He screamed in pain. "Mother fucker!" he yelled, "you little cocksucker" and swung at me with his bloody right hand now in a fist, catching me only slightly on the temple as I ducked forward. In one motion I transferred the knife to my left hand and with a forceful arching move I swung beneath his outstretched right arm and drove the blade into his right side below his ribs. Butch screamed loudly in more pain, "Oww! Shit! I'll kill you!" he bellowed and grabbed my hand holding the knife, losing control of the car. The impact of my stabbing forced his foot down in a reflex hard onto the gas pedal, we drove through the wire fence and slammed into a tree.

My backpack protected me from the dashboard but my knees took a beating. Butch didn't do so well. The crash was hard, lifting the rear of the car off the ground for a moment. Smoke and dirt filled the air around us and when it settled Butch was crushed against the steering wheel, barely conscious. He mumbled something but I couldn't make it out. My door wouldn't open so I climbed out the passenger side window but before I did I pulled my knife from Butch's side as he let out a muffled scream. It was difficult to walk with the hit my knees took but I managed. I grabbed my backpack and walked around to the driver's side. Butch was a mess, unable to move, his face bloodied, yet he still continued to play the psychopath.

"I'll…kill…you…fuck." was what I could make out. How many poor souls has this bastard hurt, I wondered? I scanned both ways up and down the long, gravel road. There was not another car in sight. I put my backpack down and pulled out my hand towel with the Jersey map on it, wrapped the hilt of the Stiletto with the towel and put the blade into the bottom of Butch's neck on his left side where his shoulder and neck met, and I shoved my knife with all I had into his neck and down into his chest. The towel instantly became red with blood but it acted as a shield, preventing his blood from splattering on me.

Butch convulsed violently but only for a few seconds and his physical movements were restricted between the seat and the steering wheel he was wedged against. When he stopped moving I grabbed the blade, keeping the towel between it and my hand, and slowly withdrew my knife from his blood stained neck. While I did that, I leaned into his car, wondering if he could hear me any longer. "Fuck. You." I whispered into his ear. Using the towel again I wiped his blood off my knife, then dropped the towel to the ground and left it there. Again I scanned the road, still no one in sight. Butch died with his eyes and mouth open, his death gaze staring up at me. I gathered my pack and walked down the gravel road to the end where we turned in from the one-lane road that ran alongside the highway. There I made a right and walked for maybe two miles until I came to a small bridge that ran over a narrow but fast moving river. It was as good a place as any to crash and getting off the road was important. Access to underneath the bridge was easy, and there was a modest patch of dirt and rock that would be my bed until the next morning. I removed my bloody clothes, emptied my backpack and stuffed the remaining contents into the cloth bag. A short distance into the water there were some large stones and finding one I could handle I overturned it and buried my bloody clothes beneath. Using my knife I cut the backpack into pieces and one-at-a-time tossed the remnants into the fast moving water. The backpack's frame I buried in several locations along the bank. When these tasks were completed and I settled down for the night, several police cars past on the bridge overhead, lights and sirens blaring.

I guessed they'd found Butch.

The morning brought cloudy skies but no rain. I cautiously found my way back to the interstate, feeling refreshed after washing in the cold waters of the river. I missed my towel. The highway seemed almost abandoned, the cars were few and far between each other, but I finally did get a ride from a trucker named Tim. Nice enough fellow, driving a large semi, hauling machine parts to a warehouse in Chicago. He shared some dry cereal with me and water that he carried in some gallon bottles behind his seat. Interesting life he'd had: was in the army, served a tour of duty in Germany, never called to Vietnam, owned a farm in Oregon but got busted growing weed. He was able to avoid jail time because of an improper search warrant but says his lawyer took most of what he had, leaving him just enough to buy this rig. Now he picks up long haul jobs, likes to be on his own on the road but occasionally will pick up a hitchhiker for the company. Told him I was grateful.

Chicago was a long way off and soon enough I fell asleep. Tim gently nudged me awake, we were pulled over to the side of the road just before a toll booth. Said he takes the exit beyond the toll and this was the best spot to let me out. I hopped down off his truck, Tim told me there was a diner down the road a few miles and wished me luck before driving off.

It was dark and very late, no way would anyone see me with my thumb out now so I walked the distance to the diner. I grabbed a booth by the front window, ordered an entire meal because I was ravished and took my time eating it knowing I had a bit of a wait before the sun came up. A cop came into the diner, walked to the counter and ordered a coffee. I could see him checking me out, wearing a dirty, buttoned-down workshirt over a pair of sweat pants. He took notice of my cloth bag and sleeping bag on the opposite seat. As he was leaving he gave me a nod hello, slightly tipping his cap at me. I returned the greeting but wasn't comfortable doing so. The cop walked to his patrol car, got on his radio but didn't leave. That was my cue and I motioned for the waitress to give me my check. It took uncomfortably long for her to write me up and I snatched the check from her hand before she could put it down. Whatever the total was didn't matter to me. I threw down a few large bills at the register and hurried out.

But it was too late.

Two more patrol cars came racing up to the diner's entrance. The steps outside ran adjacent to the building, there were no more than four or five stairs down to the parking lot. Four cops in three cars, doors flung open where they crouched behind them, with guns drawn. "Let me see your hands" they yelled, "drop what you're carrying and put your hands on your head!"

The diner steps faced east. I could see the sun coming up over the horizon casting long shadows over everything its light touched. It was higher in the sky where home was. Where my daddy was.

"Do it now!" a cop yelled, "drop the fucking bag and get on your knees" he commanded.

My hand was in the cloth bag, I flicked the switch on the stiletto. When I pulled it from the bag its shiny blade reflected the morning sun, casting a glint in the cops eyes.

"He's carrying" was the last thing I heard. The first bullet tore through my left shoulder, breaking my clavicle, causing me to drop the knife. Another went through my right thigh, a third into my gut. There were eleven shots , seven hitting me but I only felt the first three.

I fell back into a bloody heap on the top landing. Before I closed my eyes for the last time I noticed the rising sun had turned from morning orange to yellow. The heat of the sun's rays on my face were the last sensation I would experience in this life. I could hear the voices inside my head shutting down, one-by-one, until there was nothing but quiet. Then, nothing at all...

Dream Lover

Chapter I

My name is Jason Black. The story I am about to tell you is of my boyhood friend, Adam Hacker, of a mystery and an adventure. Mostly it is a tale of either a surreal dream or apocryphal reality. The reader needs to decide.

In my hands is a letter I've just received from Adam, it arrived in a small package that also contained a CD. The package was mailed from Shelby, Montana where he now resides, the CD is a recording of Adam playing with some local musicians he met in Shelby, and the music that I'm hearing is an original song Adam wrote and played the flute on. It's a live performance, taped at a local bar in the town where he lives. The letter explains the songs' meaning, but before I relay this information I think it would be pertinent to elucidate the reader on how the story got to this point.

First off, I miss Adam and have not seen him for many years; most likely I won't see him again until we meet at Hell's Gate, but there is a journey I need to bring you on so you can understand why my boyhood friend now lives more than 2200 miles away.

To begin my tale, I need to design for the reader the primary setting of where my narrative takes place. For this to happen, we need to take this journey back through history, to the Victorian era, that ran from 1837 to 1901, and, in particular, the locale of the event I am about to describe.

In the rolling hills of the Highlands Region in northeast New Jersey lies an incredible, spectacular expanse of an old Victorian mansion named Ringwood Manor. It offers passerbys, especially if traveling north on Sloatsburg Road, a breathtaking view of a marvel of 19th century architecture that looks exactly like what it is: several individual homes connected together to form one huge, imbalanced, but stately home. This odd but engrossing structural wonder was brought about by the whimsy of the last living matron of Ringwood: Sarah Amelia Hewitt. Abram and Amelia Hewitt, along with their children, were the last family to own and occupy Ringwood Manor just prior and up to the turn of the 20th century. They acquired the manor in 1854 from Amelia's father, Peter Cooper, the American industrialist, inventor, philanthropist, and one-time candidate for President of the United States. The same Peter Cooper who designed and built the first steam locomotive in the U.S., and founded the Cooper Union for the Advancement of Science and Art in Manhattan, New York City. The Hewitt's were a very wealthy family and lived, primarily, in New York. Ringwood, for all it's opulence, was their summer retreat and an occasional fall or winter holiday getaway.

Amelia (as she was known by, foregoing her given birth name of Sarah) was an eccentric woman, tending scrupulously to the needs of her family. She was the principal overseer when it came to the manor's appearance, both inside and out. Amelia would purchase nearby homes she found desirable and have them moved and attached to the existing Ringwood building. By no means was this a small feat, even by today's engineering standards. so one can safely surmise that in the late 19th century this must have proved a Herculean task. This ambitious endeavor created a design of Federal, Italianate, Neo-Greco, and neoclassical components that, put together, created the structure that is seen today.

The interior of Ringwood is inundated with collectibles of art, sculpture, and rare antique furniture that Amelia and her daughters amassed on their European sojourns. She displayed each artifact in the Manor's stately rooms and halls for her family and friends to admire, and they are still in place for visitor's today. Each individual room has it's own distinctive decor: from the music room's hand painted mural, imported from Europe, to the spacious Main Hall's classic and elaborate oaken carvings and paneling of pure Gothic revival in America. There are 28 bedrooms and 13 bathrooms, sufficient for the Hewitt's family, guests and servants. The first floor was entirely used for entertaining, with the Hewitt's bedrooms, along with their guest rooms, on the second floor. The third floor was where the servants resided. Three sprawling floors of life among the wealthy!

Abram Hewitt graduated from Columbia College where he eventually taught mathematics, and along the way earned a degree in law. He was also a former Mayor of New York City and was a successful entrepreneur before he married Amelia. A good part of his wealth was amassed from his partnerships in the iron mines that were once prevalent in New Jersey's northeast counties. The mines predated the Revolutionary War and were, at one time, available to anyone for the taking, until Hewitt and his associates of other well-to-do men purchased the land the mines were on and turned them into an enterprise. They had the foresight to realize that iron's role as a chief component in steel was vital to the then current way of life in America. In reality, the mines were not as productive as they had hoped but nonetheless they helped establish several small communities in the area solely by their utilization of necessary manpower.

Edward Cooper, Amelia's brother, was a student of Abram Hewitt at Columbia and traveled with him to Europe in 1843. On their return home one year later they were shipwrecked together and upon their rescue Abram became more of a family member to the Cooper's. This close association with the Cooper family provided the backdrop for Abram to fall in love with Edward's sister, Amelia. She found it impossible to resist his boyish good looks and refined manners while he was captivated by her beauty and charm. They were married in 1855.

Abram and Amelia remained very much in love their entire lives together, he being a good father and a kind and gentle husband, Amelia being the caring and attentive wife, dutiful to her husband and the needs of her children. It's been said that in all their married years Abram never stopped courting Amelia and she never failed to respond to his courtships like the innocent maiden that she once was during their tender, early years. Of the two of them, Abram died first in 1903.

Amelia was left to carry on. She became a stately, active woman in her later years, demanding but fair with her children, always striving to keep alive their memory of Abram and the wisdom he sought to bestow in them. To those who knew her, Amelia's stern manner could never hide the broken heart she carried over Abram's loss, and when she was much older and lay dying from the ravages of age, Abram's name was on her lips.

In 1936, Erskine Hewitt, the last surviving child of Abram and Amelia, deeded Ringwood Manor, all of its contents, and the land on which it sits to the State of New Jersey. It became a State Historical park, attracting countless visitors each year to relish the splendor of the beautifully manicured grounds and the magnificent Manor itself. To this day people marvel at the home that glorified the upper-class status the Hewitt's enjoyed.

It will bear the reader well for me to explain one more detail of Ringwood relevant to this story and it's the fact that Ringwood Manor dates back further in time than the Hewitt or Cooper families. The structure that Amelia began to add homes onto was actually the second building erected on that site. The first was built by Robert Erskine, known in history as George Washington's mapmaker during the Revolutionary War. His home was known as the Colonial Manor house, but it burned to the ground in the late 1700's. What Peter Cooper purchased was constructed by the Ryerson family in 1807. I submit this information to help you understand that there were many, many souls that have come and gone in Ringwood's long history, and as with any building this old and as occupied as it has been through the years, there are the inevitable tales of the paranormal that abound in detail concerning it's long since deceased inhabitants.

One such tale is of an old man carrying a hurricane lamp who waits on a footbridge on one of the property's many roads. He greets passersby casually and accompanies them for a short distance, walking alongside and affably engaging in their conversation. Visitors assume him to be a park employee wearing period garb until he unexplainably disappears. Some believe it is the spirit of Robert Erskine himself who is entombed in an above ground crypt nearby. The tombstone's brickwork are regularly replaced because the bricks are often found loosened from their settings and strewn on the ground. While this might be attributed to vandals or souvenir hunters, there are many who have studied the positioning of the loose bricks and have determined that they were pushed out from *within* the tomb!

Then there is the story of the gentleman garbed in Victorian attire who sits on a bench in a foyer just off the Manor's main hall. Those he addresses also assume him to be a costumed host but he too abruptly disappears when a visitor's attention is momentarily drawn elsewhere. I, myself, have spoken to a man who experienced this same event and while describing to the me the details of this occurence I must say he seemed uneasy with the memory those many years later.

In the depth's of the property's mines when they were active, miners would hear strange knockings, always before a serious accident, so when the knocking began they would immediately scurry to safety, sometimes not returning for several days until they were absolutely sure all was well or their continued employment demanded it.

Seance's inside the manor have produced documented phenomena, such as voices, footsteps, etc, but the most famous of ghost tales at Ringwood is that of the spirit that appears only when a storm is raging outside. The specter of a woman looms hovering above the middle landing of the main stairway off the Grand Hall. She floats down the stairs and straight through to a doorway on the building's east side. It's been said that this spirit is oftentimes accompanied by wails of pain and mourning from a host of voices, and the spirit itself seems to be calling for someone. Many believe it is the ghost of Amelia Hewitt calling for her husband Abram. Of all the tales of spiritual encounters at Ringwood, none of which have ever been proven factually, or for that matter, disproven, I can be as God's witness to this last apparition. This is the basis of my story and that of my friend Adam, and it bodes me well to tell others.

Chapter II

From our adolescent years, Adam Hacker and I were as brothers, closer in bond than our own natural brothers. I knew Adam as much or more than anyone on this good earth ever could, yet there was so much more to him that remained an enigma. Whatever he displayed on the outside - and to the world that persona was who Adam was - I knew there were turmoils within his soul. Unanswered questions that he never asked.

Early on, the group of people we called friends, and myself, called him "Hack", but that nickname didn't carry over into his later adolescent years. It just didn't match his dirty-blond hair, blue eyes and lean frame. Besides, he never liked the moniker from anyone other than me, but even I resorted to using his God-given Christian name, unless I really needed to get his attention.

The two of us were part of a group of young men growing up in a New Jersey suburb, most of us living within just a few blocks of each other. When young we did the things young boys did: played together, fought, got into mischief, teased girls, hated school, and pushed the limits of our parent's patience. As we grew older a line was slowly being drawn in the sand with some of us primarily involved in sports, having highly competitive spirits, while the others found the cultural aspects of living alluring, particularly as concerned art and music. Both sides of our group were very active in their pursuits and though you would think these differences would have created a conflict in our relationships, it was, in fact, that very diversity that kept us together. Though I will admit in later years it was these very same dissimilarities that separated us onto different paths.

Adam was neutral territory, he being the strongest common ground we had. He sought to excel in all the activities either side engaged in, his efforts going above and beyond what anyone expected of him. The problem was, he never actually excelled at anything, although I believe he could have, and rather easily at that. Too many serious attempts in so many directions just brought him so far in a given ability. He was the second fastest runner; one of, but not our best, musician; a great story teller but a still developing writer. Adam confided in me that he wanted to be, more than anything, a good musician and writer and I was inclined to agree with him if he would only have directed his energy towards that single, constructive goal.

Together, we were storybook friends: Tom Sawyer and Huck Finn, Bert and Ernie, Stan and Laurel. We laughed together, shared each others' triumphs and heartbreaks, mourned our losses as good friends do, and I will tell you that I was always amazed by his vivacity for life. When something had his interest, he delved into it with an intensity that surpassed all acceptable boundaries. Adam was never satisfied until he knew all there was to know about the object of his obsession. When addressed on the matter he became nervous, a man who would talk too fast, and his speech belied his intelligence.

By his late teens, after his awkward physical years had passed, Adam grew into a handsome young man. Tall, blue-eyed with dark blonde hair, he made sure he kept himself in shape, always conscious of his appearance. He had a distinct voice, the type of speech that made each and every word he uttered in perfect clarity. Often, when excited, he spoke too fast, but he was always understood. What stood out to me was how he held onto to his baby face looks even into his late teens and early twenties. The ladies seemed taken by his boyish charms and good looks but Adam was always a one-woman man, staying in a relationship until the well ran dry and both parties moved on. Usually it was amicable. Usually.

There was one woman who Adam regretted losing, and maybe he could have repaired any damage done but that wasn't his style. Instead he asked me to take a ride with him to no where in particular; would help him clear his mind, he said. It became a casual Sunday afternoon drive, touring though the countryside in the mountains of northern New Jersey when we saw it: Ringwood Manor. The building came unexpectedly into our view and from the road we couldn't help but marvel at the spectacular vista; this large multi-architectural wonder sitting atop a hillside overlooking a marvelously well manicured landscape. We were intrigued enough to enter through its gates, exploring the grounds and eventually the Manor and its many rooms. To tell you Adam was mesmerized by what we were seeing would be undermining what he was experiencing. After a few hours we left but I could not say how many times after that first visit Adam returned to Ringwood, but it was more than a few times.

I do know it was more often than I thought reasonable, and maybe considered obsessive.

But Adam was an extremist. It was built into his DNA, part of his persona. In what was typical fashion for Adam he familiarized himself with the history of every room, every wall and ceiling, each piece of furniture, art and sculptures, whether they were located within the Manor or somewhere among the many acres of the park where the Manor sat. He could recite it's history, both factual and false, truth or rumored and though I thought it strange information for anyone to retain to such a degree I must admit he could impress virtually anyone with his diatribes about Ringwood's humble beginnings on through it's place among New Jersey's historically preserved landmarks. Adam was especially fond of regaling all with his stories of Ringwood's paranormal history, it's sightings, the unaccountable sounds of voices and horse-drawn carriages, the ghostly spectres that some claimed to have encountered. He knew, in detail, the story behind all of them, unraveling his tales as if he was reciting from a novel.

He was explicit with the particulars of the Hewitt family history, especially of Amelia Cooper-Hewitt. Adam would expel recounts of her that dazzled his listeners, many who couldn't believe this man could retain such minute facts of such an obscure figure from America's past. It was information he gathered that must have required hours of sifting through countless piles of research material, library visits, thumbing through endless amounts of archival memos and photographs. And this was all before the days of the Internet. It was nothing short of obsession but if you knew Adam you would have understood this to be within the parameters of his personality. He fixated over details of what caught his interest because - at least from my perspective - to make up for the fly-by-night attitude he had over so many ventures during his earlier years.

On a day that I will never forget, Adam came to me with a plan, so absurd in structure, so devoid of common reasoning, yet it required my assistance to complete, that even to this day I am bewildered by my having agreed to participate. He told me that he and another mutual friend, John Thomas (whom we called JT) were going to spend an overnight in Ringwood Manor, said they had a foolproof plan to pull this stunt off and get out without anyone the wiser. Obviously this scheme was without the consent of the park's rangers or the Manor's curator and there could be dire consequences if they were caught. All this did not go unmentioned by me when he told of what they wanted to do. Adam explained the Manor's internal security was simply beam sensors set low in certain doorways and all the windows. Sensors connected by a beam of light that if interrupted would set both an external alarm and internal direct to the ranger station located at the Manor's eastern wing. The door alarms were primarily to keep visitors from crossing the threshold of the doorways on the second and third floors, the window alarms were to keep intruders out when the museum was closed. He explained the doorway alarms could easily be averted if someone were already inside when the Manor's doors closed for the evening. It didn't escape his notice that there were no doorway alarms on the first floor or on any of the staircases, nor in any of the hallways. Adam knew where each and every beam sensor was located. These same hallways were illuminated with low intensity security lights that remained lit during the night, allowing anyone to wander heedlessly through the Manor.

My help was needed to drive Adam and JT to Ringwood late in the day. As the park closed, we would enter the Manor only if there were visitors already inside. Adam and JT would straddle behind a group on the second floor, and when this group moved on, they would hide in a bedroom Adam meticulously chose due to it's beam sensor being set so low. The both of them would step over the beam and hide beneath the large four-poster canopy bed against the far wall to the left of the doorway. Meanwhile I would "join" the group that we previously straddled and leave with them, assuming any ranger who sees people enter and exit everyday could never recollect anything more than my being familiar. Two less people among a group of visitors should not even occur to him or her, but they also had to hope the group leaving, minus the small backpacks Adam and JT carried in with them, would not be noticed.

Why Adam never asked me to partake in this adventure beyond merely a diversion never arose. I am certain he knew I wouldn't go along with it, at least as far as trespassing on state property, but he also knew I would attempt to dissuade him in this nefarious endeavor. Of course, I asked him why and what did he hope to accomplish with this action? I again explained the possible charges if they were caught, not to mention the danger of wandering around an old building barely lit, but I think it was only to hear me talk so I could say "I told you so" should they get caught.

" I want proof", Adam said,"proof of the dead's disembodied spirits that Ringwood lays claim to. Imagine what we could do with such evidence?"

But I couldn't imagine. Even if they were successful in capturing anything the world was far too skeptical of the paranormal for it to be of any value, but Adam didn't see it that way. He and JT carried cameras, infrared detectors, small flashlights and recorders to document the legends of Ringwood's hauntings, if indeed they did exist. Adam was certain they did.

Chapter III

Really, I don't know why I agreed to this nonsensical plan, but I did. Adam owned me during these years, that's the only sane reason I can rationalize as to my participation. At first, my refusal was adamant, based on the disbelief of Adam's seriousness at going through with it, but I weakened with his persistence and we planned a time to leave and a time I would return the next morning to pick them up. Adam outlined their entire evening to me, explaining they would be back at their hiding spots before the Manor doors opened and just as they got in, they would get out: wait for a group to walk through the second floor and leave the building as nothing more than visitors.

The day finally came, it was a Friday and we were on the road shortly after noon. Adam was like a child on his way to visit a carnival for the first time. He talked excitedly about what he expected was going to happen, planned different camera shots to capture any wandering spirits and he mimicked the sounds he anticipated the recorder would capture. Meanwhile, and outside of Adam's noticing, JT was turning a pale shade of white, remaining strangely quiet. After we arrived within sight of the Manor JT couldn't contain himself any longer and offered his eleventh hour retreat to Adam's plan.

"It's alright, JT", was all Adam said, almost as if he expected it. We parked in the lot, drank coffee and waited for the next wave of visitors. With the practiced nonchalance we worked on, we lagged slightly behind a group of five people. In the Manor we always kept a room between them and us, taking pictures of the artwork and sculptures, doing our best to not draw any notice. When this group entered the west side staircase, we scurried to the one at the opposite side of the Manor. At the second floor landing, we saw them at the far end of the long hallway, peering into the bedrooms and sitting parlors roped off to the public. Our pace was set to meet them outside the bedroom where Adam planned his concealment. We even greeted them with a hello which they respectfully returned. At that point, we began taking pictures of the room and others nearby, keeping an eye on the group as they neared the staircase to head back down (the third floor wasn't open to public viewing). In a flash, Adam stepped over the security beam carrying his equipment, gave me a wink along with a thumbs-up and slid under the high bed. It had a large quilt draped over it that extended to the floor, preventing any visual beneath it, and the foot of the bed was solid oak from its canopy top to the floor. I knew it was useless but I queried Adam one last time.

"Dude, you sure that you want to…?"

"Jason", he interrupted, "I'll see you in the morning. Don't let me down, buddy."

JT and me raced to descend the staircase just behind the group that was already near the bottom. Having the two of us leaving, in retrospect, was certainly less distracting than if I was by myself. The museum's curator thanked us for coming as he prepared to close up the Manor for another day. I had this strong sense of foreboding I couldn't shake, could feel my anxiety increasing as we left the Manor and headed for the parking lot. I turned to look up at the window of the bedroom where my friend was hiding when against the far wall of the room I saw a beam of light quickly race across my visual. "Adam", I thought, "you crazy bastard.".

After dropping JT off and returning home, I spent an uneasy and restless evening, sleeping only occasionally throughout the long night. I do remember one dream that startled me awake: roused by screams that shattered the stillness of the night. The screams were coming from inside Ringwood Manor and I was outside, below the bedroom window where Adam was, but my feet were leaden, not allowing me to move. Soon, the screams were behind me and within moments they were enveloping me. That's when I awoke, sweating profusely.

There was no way sleep was possible after that nightmare, and because it was a long drive and I wanted to get this insanity over with I started for Ringwood before dawn. It wasn't until the Manor came into my view that I realized how early I was; there were more than a few hours before the doors opened to visitors. I couldn't help but notice how quiet and serene the park was so early before throngs of people showed up. Having had so little sleep, combined with the stillness and the clean mountain air, my thermos of coffee came in handy. Caffeine became my friend, keeping me conscious until the appointed hour.

Rather than sit in my car and wait for both the Manor to open and visitors to arrive, I decided to take a walk to the front door and stroll along the grounds within sight of the main entrance, but when I walked past the ranger station and turned right towards the building's entrance, a confusing sight awaited me. There was Adam, outside the main entrance, sitting on his heels on the lawn, arms folded over his knees and staring at the second floor window of the bedroom where I left him. I stopped when I saw him, wanted to make sure he wasn't where he was because that's where a ranger told him to remain, but when I realized it was only him and me, I approached.

"Adam", I called. But he did not respond.

Again I repeated his name and again, no response. I stood over my friend, put my hand on his shoulder, and now with a worried voice I asked:

"Adam, are you okay?"

His equipment lay on the ground next to where he was squatting. His eyes were cold, distant, with a vacant stare, intent only on the bedroom window of this old Victorian mansion. From where I stood every door and window appeared solidly shut, and climbing down from a second story window of this old building would have been reckless, but here was Adam, here was my long-time friend sitting outside the place he was locked in the night before. Something had gone wrong.

Abruptly, Adam stood up and finally spoke:

"Nothing, Jason... it was all for nothing" and he began to walk towards the parking lot, leaving everything he brought along on the ground by my feet.

"But how…?" I started to ask, but Adam would not answer or react to my bafflement. Could the fact he encountered no spiritual icons of Ringwood's past have been that much of a disappointment? And the question remained: how did he get outside? I gathered his equipment and joined him at my car. Not a word was exchanged between us, Adam slept on the ride home leaving me with no clue as to what happened. When we arrived at his house he simply said thanks and took what belonged to him. As he was walking up the steps to his house I called out, sounding a little mad, but more concerned. I had questions and believed I deserved answers.

"Talk to me, Hack. What happened last night? How did you get out?"

"Nothing happened at all" he said, sitting down on the top step to his front door, "Ringwood is just an empty, deserted mansion. When the sun came up, I found a window on the west side with no alarm and let myself out. Locked it behind me." I don't think he realized how unlikely this story sounded but I wasn't going to push the issue. It would have been useless.

"I'll call you later, Jason. Just need some sleep". He rose from his seat and headed up the stairs to his home. I was not satisfied with how this meeting ended, his excuse seemed rehearsed. Now I was feeling even more than a bit angry and wasn't sure why. Think I still wanted more after my willful participation in this excursion.

" I need more than this", I shouted at him before he had the chance to close his front door,"makes no sense to me how you got out of the manor. What the hell happened last night?".

He could tell I was angry, but stood there silently in the doorway. After a few moments, moments during which I could hear the early songs of birds, feel the coolness of the morning breeze, he spoke to me.

" I will tell you, Jason. I will explain all that happened but I am asking you as my friend that you wait until I am ready. Then you will learn everything that occurred last night. As your friend, I give you my word. I am just asking for some time".

That was it then, I knew this discussion was over. I sensed that neither my anger of feeling excluded, or even if I pleaded with Adam, there was nothing more to be said. This wasn't the Adam I knew, not that day and from that day on. He was no longer the boyhood friend who shared the intimacy of his life as I did mine with him, the one whom I called brother. The man I knew had disappeared somewhere inside, or was stolen from me, lost in the hallways of Ringwood Manor.

In the coming months I was hard-pressed to believe he still considered me his friend. He no longer returned my calls, avoiding socializing with me, or anyone else, whenever possible. Adam became a different person, someone I hadn't met before and it seemed he needed no one in his life now. When, on those rare occasions we were together, Ringwood was never a subject that was broached. He avoided the discussion, the enthusiasm he once carried about it and so vividly displayed was gone. His avoidance of addressing what happened that night became an enigma for myself and anyone else who knew Adam.

One thing didn't change, in fact it was magnified in it's intensity, was Adam spending more time at the Manor than he ever did before. His weekends, days off from work, any free time Adam had was spent wandering the Manor halls and grounds, taking countless number of pictures. In his room, his desk and floor were overspread with books, magazine clippings and photos of Ringwood. The printed matter particularly addressed the history of the Manor, especially the Hewitt family history. Adam became a member of Ringwood's Historical Society, contributing generously to the museum's fund for it's preservation in both money and his time spent at events designed to raise funds for the same. In summary, he became entangled with Ringwood Manor in very conceivable way possible. It was his life now, his reason to exist, and I was left with no clue as to why.

Chapter IV

The Historical Society would present a Christmas gala each year at the manor. They elaborately and painstakingly decorated the entire first floor, room-by-room, in a Victorian mode to display how the Hewitt's themselves might have done the same in their home at a turn-of-the-century holiday season. Adam became thoroughly enamored of this project, his contribution being to present the Hewitt dining room to all visitors. He was a good public speaker, waxing eloquently to each group a brief history of the room's furniture, explaining each individual pieces history, from the large sideboard to the dining room table, even the tableware. His oration detailed what a Hewitt holiday meal for them and their guests would have consisted of. Adam knew the mannerisms and expected mores of all those sitting down to dine, even the explicit responsibilities of each servant. What was baffling to me was that he was able to cite what he claimed were discussions being held at the holiday table, quoting people like Adam Hewitt, Peter Cooper, or several of their guests. Even the Manor's curator seemed astonished that Adam could have researched and obtained such minute and detailed information. As with the rest of us, the curator assumed much of what Adam said was the output of a creative mind, mixing fact with fiction.

During these presentations Adam was the man I once knew. He was no longer the introvert he had come to be, he was, instead, a cornucopia of energy, his eagerness for the material was on parade! But when the Victorian Christmas show was completed he again assumed the role of being no more than a casual acquaintance, a familiar face from my past of someone I once held in high esteem.

Now, as I consider myself a man who has never been known to exaggerate, what is to follow makes it important that I emphasize this point so that you understand I am of sound mind an body, and was from this moment of time I am about to relate and hopefully, I can avow, from then to now.

It was late during a cool Fall evening. I had called it a day when Adam paid me an unexpected visit, appearing edgy and very uneasy in his demeanor. He came into my home and asked if it was okay if he lit a cigarette. Adam never smoked as long as I knew him so this was a surprise request, but I agreed to allow it if it helped calm his stressful comportment.

"Jason, I'm sorry to bother this late, but I need to talk to you. Please" was the first words Adam said. Initially I might have been apprehensive. It had been a long time since Adam sought my confidence and I developed the impression our once strong bond of friendship had passed us by sometime back, but as it was years ago I could never stay angry with this man who shared my childhood adventures with me.

"Adam, c'mon in. Have a seat and I'll make coffee. We can shoot the breeze as long as you'd like". I returned with the coffee and found him fidgeting on his chair's edge, already into this second cigarette. "So, what's happening, buddy?" I said light-heartedly, trying to ease the moment for him, but his serious demeanor was not to be subdued. He then proceeded to tell me the most incredible tale.

"Jason, what I need to tell you I've never told anyone, and maybe, of all people I should have opened up to you sooner. I have tried to live with this for a long time and made a judgement it was best that way... but now it has become hard to live with. Listen, Jason, you won't think I'm crazy will you?" Tough call, was it a rhetorical question? I've always considered Adam to be somewhat off-center, but accepted it as a condition of his creative and restless mind. Regardless, it seemed time to calm him down and assure him, no matter what, I would accept what he had to tell me as gospel. I told him to continue with this story, I would make no judgement. He seemed a bit calmed by my reply, collected himself and continued:

"After my overnight stay at Ringwood I told you nothing had happened, but something did happen, Jason. Something incredible and so unbelievable that I've spent these last few years trying to convince myself that is was only a dream, that I had fallen asleep under that big bed…". Adam paused, lit another cigarette, then continued with his story: "You see, when I was hiding under the bed, waiting for the guard to make his final round, I fell asleep. I have no idea how long I slept, I just recall waking up and become startled by the now unfamiliarity of my location, the smell of the room had changed, the *feeling* was different. Within moments I gathered my thoughts and remembered why I was there. It was very dark and I felt for my watch to find out how long I'd been out, but there was no watch on my wrist. Damn, I thought, I could have sworn I put it on earlier, how stupid could I have been? I reached out to my side on the floor for my backpack which had the flashlight inside, but my backpack was missing also. This was ridiculous, I thought, as I struggled to avoid panic. I know the pack was there, it had to be, but as hard as I tried searching for it, feeling my way around in the pitch black, I could not find it! I needed to gather my bearings and start over again so I crawled out from under the bed ever so quietly since I had no idea if the guard had been through or not. Once out and on my feet I was sure I would be able to locate my bag…but it was so damn dark. I couldn't even detect the security light across the bedroom doorway or the hallway's night lights in the blackness. I moved very slowly and cautiously towards the doorway because it was all I could do to distinquish the shadowy forms of furniture in the room that was reflecting barely visible light from a full-moon outside.

"Something was different, very different. Even the quiet of the night's darkness was new to me. What I noticed again was the odor in the air. It was not the Manor's usually stale odor but rather it was fresh, fresh pine and, maybe, oak. There were other aromas I didn't recognize but it was all so clean smelling.

'Stupid' I found myself saying out loud because I didn't carry the flashlight on my belt.

"Then the noises came. Noises from outside, terrifying at first that froze me where I stood. The sounds I heard didn't make any sense: it sounded like the clomping of horses' feet, with another noise that could only be described as carriage wheels. My curiousity came to the surface and I edged slowly towards the window, keeping myself alert should reason arise that necessitated my scurrying under thebed, when I heard a voice, a distinctly clear woman's voice coming from the stairwell at the end of the hall outside the room I was in. 'Abram?' the voice called loudly, 'are you coming dearest?' "

I dared not move.

"'Please come now, Abram. Our guests are all here'. There was no logic or reasoning left in my soul at that point, Jason. Nothing made any sense. I should have been, from sheer terror, fleeing from that room, fleeing from the Manor... but that voice! Something responded inside of me that allowed only a few short moments to compose my thoughts and I moved through the room and out into the hallway. I became completely unconscious of the doorway alarm which only after I had passed through the portal did I notice it was no longer there.

" 'Abram, we can't start without you. Won't you answer me?' the woman's voice pleaded. The stairway down to the Main Hall was now only a few steps to my right. The voice I heard came from the bottom of the stairs on the first floor, out of my view because the stairs made a 180-degree turn after the middle landing. I turned towards the other end of the hallway and I realized that from where I stood to the opposite end, any illumination was coming from a few gas lamps hanging on the walls of the hallway! Lamps were lit and working and I was certain they were not there earlier. I saw no trace of the night security lights.

" 'Abram, I hear you there, dearest' , the woman's voice called again, 'hurry now, or father will be angry'.

"Once again my legs could not move from fear and I could feel my heart beating in my chest so loudly I was sure this woman calling could hear it too. Gathering my wits, I was able to continue moving forward: slowly to the top of the stairs, then four steps down to the landing. There I came upon a mirror that hung on the wall to my left. Jason, what I saw…the overwhelming shock…will be with me forver. The image in the mirror was not me! It was Abram Hewitt! Convinced I was seeing his ghost I gasped, falling back against the banister, but I noticed the reflection in the mirror did the same. After a moment I straightened up slowly and again the image copied my every movement. Inquisitively now, I raised my right hand to my chin and was mimicked by the mirror's personification. How could this be? I moved close to the reflective surface and there staring back was a young Abram Hewitt, his strong, stern face recognizable to me from countless photographs and drawings I'd see of the Hewitt family.

"This reflection brought yet another shock: it was my clothes. I was not wearing any of the clothes I came to Ringwood with, instead I was adorned with a dark brown tweed double-breasted suit, from a straight-up collar down to a pair of 19th century gentlemen's side button boots. Victorian apparel that Abram Hewitt would have worn was now on me, and damned if I didn't notice these clothes a few moments before.

"After I came to terms with this latest revelation, I became aware of the woman who was standing at the bottom of the steps leading to the first floor, so I…".

"Wait a minute, Adam", I interrupted, and God knows why I waited so long to do so, "what are you telling me here? A dream? You are talking about a dream, right? I mean, you're awfully distraught over this and maybe that's why you need to get it out of your system, need me to hear it for what it is. I'm right about that, aren't I?" My voice rose in pitch in a unconscious attempt to express my frustration at trying to believe what I was hearing, but Adam sat quietly, his expression telling me that he expected this reaction, that he was prepared for it. He sipped his now cold coffee, lit another cigarette. In my room's low light I could see his deep, blue eyes penetrating my soul as if searching for an answer to my outburst, or maybe he was trying to find that trust in my soul he was convinced was there when he arrived here earlier. He then spoke in a whisper that sounded so pleading:

"Jason, I can only hope it was a dream, but my heart pleads for its reality. I don't know how to explain it anymore than how it happened". He paused again, then continued, taking a deep breath before exhaling a long, low sigh. "What stood below me on the landing... was an angel, an angel of the morning. A precious, cherished gem that you keep forever, no matter what. I was a few feet away from Amelia Hewitt. Not a ghost or an exaggeraton of my imagination, but Amelia in the flesh and blood as a young, beautiful woman. Jason, I felt no fear or trepidation, caution was not a word I knew then. It was as if that moment was all I expected it to be, and how could I have ever expected such a thing?

" 'Silly goose, there you are', Amelia said, 'come to dinner. Father and the guests have been waiting anxiously for your arrival, out of nothing more than hunger, I am sure." I descended the steps to the first floor where Amelia took my hand.' We must not keep them waiting any further, but first...', and she kissed me lightly and lovingly. Jason, it felt so real, so natural. How could it be so vivid, or such realism exist in a dream? This was a vibrant Amelia, alive and so very much in love with me it coursed through my veins at her touch. It belied my senses as to what was occurring, especially at the taste of her sweet lips. Everything I could see was not as it was the day before. The lighting was either from outside or from gas lamps. The visitor's desk was gone and there were servants scurrying about everywhere. Fireplaces were roaring to parlay the nip I now felt in the air. Amelia led me to the dining room where people were seated around the table. All the conversations in the room stopped and all eyes were cast my way when I came into the room with Amelia.

" 'Ah, Master Hewitt. It is good you have decided to join us for dinner. At long last! We thought , for the while, the lot of us would leave tonight that much thicker in our waists having to share the rich meal you would have neglected. Our guest's horses would have been none the happier for it!', an older man said as he pat me on the back. The seated guests all laughed in appreciation.

" 'Father', Amelia said, 'for all the times I have made poor Abram wait, it is only fair that occasionally he pay me in kind'. *Father* , she called him, Jason. The man who spoke was Peter Cooper. *The* Peter Cooper, the man who owned Ringwood along with Abram Hewitt. The same man who was the founder of New York's Cooper-Union Institute. I must have looked foolish to him then, staring the way I did. A servant approached us and led us to our seats : I was seated to the right of Amelia. As we sat down, Peter Cooper raised a glass from the table, rose to his feet and spoke to his guests:

" 'Before we begin, it bodes me well to proudly be the bearer of salutations for my daughter, Amelia, and her companion, Master Abram Hewitt, who has approached me, seeking my approval for my daughter's hand in marriage and to forthwith I have given my uncompromised consent. By God's grace, may their marriage be long and prosperous, and blessed with both love and many children'.

" 'Your grandchildren!' another man quickly added, and the rest of the men in the room gave a hearty 'hear-hear' while the women politely clapped their approval. Amelia cuddled my right arm, leaned over and bussed my cheek lightly. I looked into her eyes, her loving smile whispering into my heart. Jason, I sat there so elated, ecstatic, such as I have never known, and it was there I suddenly thought of you. Though it felt so unlikely, so out-of-place that you should come into my thoughts just then, I wondered what the hell you would have rationalized about all of this. You were the bridge to my reality, so a bit of panic set in when I realized where I was, and who I was supposed to be, among so many unfamiliar faces, all long ago passed on, but who proffered to know me well. My senses became muddled, everything began to slow down, and I now expected to wake up under the bed on the second floor where once again I'd find myself in the dark amid the restored and preserved environ of Ringwood Manor as it is today.

" Except, I didn't wake up. I wanted to stay where I was right then and there, with Amelia. I couldn't tell you why, Jason, but it was she who had always been there in the recesses of my soul. If this was a dream, then let it go on. I *needed* for it to go on!

"And it did."

Chapter V

Adam reached for his jacket and laid it across his lap, a sign he was preparing to leave. He figured I'd heard enough but he couldn't have been more wrong. "It did? It did what?" I asked as intently as I could manage without expressing my frustration that he was considering ending this evening without finishing his story. Adam appeared so solemn in the quiet between us that followed, so much in pain. He tried to hide the mask of a broken but some, like myself, easily recognize that mask on another individual.

"Jason, I didn't wake up then." He startled me by both his abrupt continuation and by what he said: "I didn't wake up then, or any time soon after that. I lived the rest of Abram Hewitt's life. I married my sweet Amelia, made love to her, waited outside the room each time our midwives helped her bear me children.

" I was at the bedside of Peter Cooper when he left this world, and by the side of my own father, I mean Abram's father, John, when he passed at eighty-three years of age. There were the mines in and around Ringwood of which I held partnership in with several others, including my brother-in-law Edward. The same Edward Cooper whom I was shipwrecked with on a journey home from Europe, stranded on a lonely island until we were rescued.

"I lived through my election to both becoming the Mayor of New York City and as a member of Congress. New York was where Amelia and I lived most of our lives together.

"With Amelia, I traveled to Europe and elsewhere, giving her whatever she wanted. I never dreamed I could be so much in love. Because of Amelia, I forgot about this world where I came from. I forgot about you, Jason. The memory of this life became dimmer as the years past. I could tell you every detail of Abram Hewit's life. I knew his aches and pains, his victories and his losses. I was intimate with the man as himselft because I was the man, living his life.

"With the passing of time I grew old as Abram and became ill. I knew I was dying. It was then I remembered, began wondering if now I would wake up under the bed on the second floor of the Manor where so long ago I lay hidden. On my deathbed, Ameia sat diligently, day after day, by my side, holding my hand. I fell into and out of consciousness and always she was there, the two of us had grown old together and now I would leave first. This brought contentment to my heart. 'I will wait for you, Amelia' I told her, 'be it with my heart and soul, even if all eternity should pass before us, I will be with you again, my dearest, dearest Amelia', and as Abram Hewitt, I died."

Adam waited for a response from me but at first I could offer none. Throughout his whole story I tried, with difficulty as you can imagine, keeping an open mind and I thought I was doing well until he told me he died as Abram Hewitt. How would you react?

"As you can imagine," Adam continued, "it was here that I woke up, but I wasn't under the bed. I was outside, my watch was back on my wrist and my backpack was alongside me. I again had to gather my bearings as to where I was. This time it was more difficult because how I got outside and how I was back to this life, I have no idea. When my eyes opened I found myself sitting-up, leaning against a tree on the property some fifty yards away and facing the Manor. I was soaked in a cold sweat, dawn was just breaking. I knew the park rangers would be there soon, but I desperately wanted back inside. Every door was locked, every first floor window was sealed. How could I have gotten outside? I didn't know what to do and ran frantically from door to window until I collapsed from exhaustion. I gathered my backpack and sat down by the main entrance where you found me. Before you arrived, I realized it would be easy to break the glass on the front door or a window and race upstairs. I knew the alarms would be set off but I figured I would be gone by the time anyone got there, returned again to the past to start over again with Amelia. I hesitated and the futility of my actions took seed before I acted upon them. Where would l go? They would have found me quivering under the bed on the second floor and that wasn't what I wanted then.

"So I sat where I was, fixing my eyes on the second floor windows hoping for a glimpse of...I don't know what...maybe a glimpse of Amelia. I prayed for her to appear and tell me it was going to be alright, tell me *this* was the dream. That's when you found me."

Chapter VI

It was late and Adam wanted to leave. There wasn't anything I could think of to say that might lessen his obvious anguish, or ease the pain he was feeling. I politely offered him the possibility that it might have been no more than an intense dream.

"A dream?" he responded, "I live everyday now trying to convince myself it was a dream, a very real dream in which I lived another man's life, fell in love with this other man's wife and died an old man in his bed, as him. I just can't get myself to believe it was only a dream".

"Adam, what else could it have been?" I replied. "As your friend I am asking you to realize that this thing that is overwhelming you was no more than a very intense and magnified dream, and nothing more. The laws of logic defy it to be anything more than what it is." I tried to sound both sympathetic and adamant as I thought the moment called for, but there was no expression of acknowlegement on Adam's face. By now, he was standing and preparing to open my door to leave, nodding slightly in reluctant agreement at what I said. He didn't leave before telling me one last thing:

"Jason, Ringwood's Victorian Christmas display begins in a few weeks and you know I'm involved again. Please don't be angry, but I volunteered you as a participant. I need you to do this for me. As my friend I need you nearby, but I will understand if you don't want to do it."

Maybe because the hour was late, or this incredible evening was ending, I don't know, but I was neither angry or surprised. I sensed he truly wanted me with him for his journey to continue, so I meekly agreed.

"Oh, what the hell", I said, "let's go for it!" and we arranged the date and time I would pick him up. His eyes showed all the appreciation they could express. He gave me a simple nod and closed the door behind him on his way out.

I was 4:01 am.

Chapter VII

Preparing Ringwood Manor's first floor, adorning every room to represent the Christmas holiday during the late 1800's, was more hectic than I would have imagined. The initial group of visitors waited anxiously to be let in to begin their tour and admire the beautiful Christmas decor. I have to admit I was impressed with what the local women's club accomplished, embellishing the Manor with such wonderful Victorian flavor. I relented to the spirit of the occasion by agreeing to wear a gray turn-of-the-century servant's outfit someone found me. A bit snug and too short at the pant leg but nonetheless rich in appearance, especially for the atmosphere. I was to greet people at the main door and keep a count of how many visitors entered throughout the day.

Adam chose to wear a suit very similar to what he described he was wearing in his story when he first met Amelia Hewitt. He was assigned to the dining room and was meticulously prepared for the inquisitive throngs. Each time the room was shoulder-to-shoulder of anxious visitors, he presented his brief piece of Victorian holiday dining history. Adam would explain how the dining room was part of the Manor's north-wing section and at one time belonged to another home on the Hewitt property, added on in 1878 under the loving direction of Amelia Hewitt. He detailed what the room's paneling was made from, as well as the furniture in the room. Adam outlined the role of the servants, as well as the protocol the guests were expected to follow. Visitors were awed by the explanation that a holiday meal for the Hewitt family could easily consist of twelve courses and he listed each possible item that was prepared for dinner. Finally, Adam ended his oration by explaining it was customary for the ladies to retire to the drawing room while the men stayed behind to discuss the affairs of the day.

It was easy to notice how Adam's oration was the highlight of the tour. So many were impressed by his attention to detail and ability to answer any inquiry he received. With this year's oration Adam was approached by the Manor's curator who inquired how he could have know about some of the particulars he spoke of, such as the engagement announcement of Abram Hewitt and Amelia Cooper, or the business decision between Abram Hewitt and Edward Cooper? The curator himself worked in the Manor for twenty-three years and knew its history well, having, in fact, written a few books on the subject. He told Adam he had never come across such information in all his research. Adam replied that he didn't recall the exact source but he would be glad to forward the curator a copy of the material when he returned home. This seemed to satisfy the curator for the time being, but I knew what the truth was and wondered how Adam would handle any further inquiries from the curator or anyone else in the future.

The weather outside was making a concerted effort to hamper the day's festivities. An impending storm lingered, making the day overcast from the beginning and it rained in short interludes. It was a hard, cold rain. This made the time between groups of visitors longer, but still it was a sizable turnout. I recall taking a break from my duties as doorman. The clock said 3:10pm and I decided to pay a visit to Adam in the dining room as I noticed no visitors there. I knew he hadn't taken a break himself yet today, even at the insistence of the senior members of the Women's Club. I figured now was as good a time as any to pull him away for a short respite.

"Let's take five, Adam. We'll go grab a smoke", but he seemed uninterested. He continued to replace fresh candles in the room's candelabras.

"I can't, Jason, not now. I have to stay here…I won't leave now" he answered, almost in a gruff tone and I appeased him by not pressing the issue.

"No problem, my friend. I'll keep you company for a…" when it was that moment Adam and I and everyone else in the Manor became aware of a low, humming sound. It was a distant noise at first but continued to grow in stature with each moment. The rain oustside increased in intensity, the torrential downpour adding to the ever-increasing din of the strange noise.

Out from the back room came the curator, tailed by the show's organizers, and all in a desparate search for the source of the noise which continued to escalate in intensity. Adam and I left the dining room and amble into the Main Hall. We found the visitors beginning to leave, not knowing what the humming was but aware that it was now physically vibrating the walls themselves. The volunteers were escorting people outside. There was murmuring that the area was experiencing an earthquake, but having lived through a few myself I can tell you this was very different.

Now the hum was terrifyingly loud! More and more people scurried out of the building. If the direction of the sound could be determined, it was coming from above, from the second or third floor of the Manor. Panic began to ensue, then someone screamed! Everyone's attention was drawn to the scream: a woman at the bottom of the stairway. She pointed to the landing between the first and second floors and there, in plain view, in inexplicable horror, hovering ABOVE the landing was a specter, a ghostly spirit of a woman wearing white and flowing clothing, with long, unkempt hair. She was shrouded in a veil of translucent light. She did not move, just hovered in one spot. The humming noise had now become a chorus of wailing and moaning voices, so loud and frightening that those present felt there were in the domain of Hell itself.

Most people fled, some stood frozen in fear while others cowered to the floor, covering their eyes or their ears. I recall both men and women screaming in nothing less than abject terror. I could not move, transfixed near the dining room door. Adam stood a few feet from me, further out into the Main Hall. The stairway was directly ahead of us with the apparition no more than twenty feet away. It began to move, floating forward with outstretched arms, and began a descent downwards and directly towards Adam. It spoke in a voice that all heard above the riotous mayhem that was ensuing, speaking in a hauntingly, mystical tone:

"Abram, there you are dearest. I've been waiting", the spectre sounded, heading straight for Adam. I yelled for him to move but he did exactly the opposite. Adam stood still, waiting for the spirit to reach him with his arms outstretched in anticipation of its touch. With my legs shaking from fear I still somehow found the strength to move towards Adam, yelling all the time for him to get the hell out of there. I was finally within his reach when I heard him call out:

"Amelia…at last you've come. Take me with you, my love", and at that moment she ws upon him. I couldn't let this happen, not to my friend. I found the ability to move and move quickly, leaping through the air and tackling Adam away from the specter's open arms. We both rolled to the floor. I was beneath Adam, wrestling for control with him on top of me, trying to break free of my grasp. "NO!" he yelled, "YOU BASTARD, LET ME GO. LET ME GO, JASON".

I pleaded with Adam to listen to reason, a reasoning that I had no sense of where I was pulling it from: "It was a dream, goddammit" I yelled. "You have to see that, it was just a dream". The ghostly figure of Amelia Hewitt was directly above us, hovering in the air and continuing her reach for Adam who was still within my grip. Soon, she engulfed the both of us. "Abram", her haunting, cavernous voice spoke.

Chapter VIII

I found myself alone, blinding white light in every direction. I felt the ability to move but I could not determine any substance to my body. If there was a physical sense, it was the type you feel attempting to move through water.

There was the sensation that I was no longer in the Manor, at least as far as I could tell. Instead I was moving though the white light that began to slowly dissipate, creating a perspective of distance yet all the time remaining formless. "Adam", I yelled but no word left my mouth, instead I heard my shouting only in my thoughts, rather as a memory. I called again, concentrating with all the energy I could muster and this time my voice reverberated loudly all around me, echoing back from everywhere around me, and from nowhere:

"Not you, Jason. Not now!". Simple and clear, bellowing from Adam, but I could not ascertain the direction it came from. Without warning I was shoved from behind and I began falling rapidly through the surrounding white that now formed a horizon before me, a horizon that never got closer. My senses were reeling, and instinctively I tried to lift my arms towards my face, feeling a need to break my fall. The sensation was that I was traveling at an incredible speed such as I had never experienced, but I felt no wind on my face, no rushing of air. It was as if my surroundings were moving past me and I stood motionless.

Then WHAM!

I landed hard on the Manor's floor, my arms were up over my head still in a protective stance. I was stunned from the impact but fought losing consciousness, finding myself back in the Main Hall, almost alone since most had fled in terror. The hosts of voices where still there, continuing their wailing and the light was the ghost of Amelia Hewitt was no longer translucent, but was now a blinding, oblong oval of a non-transparent white glow. It remained hovering above the floor where Adam and I struggled, but now it was much larger in its dimensions, looming in a circular path around the entire room.

Quickly I scanned the room for Adam but to no avail. I called his name again and again and each time I yelled the wailing voices bellowed louder as if to intentionally drown me out. God, I thought, this can't be happening. Adam was still in the light with that thing, still in the grasp of Amelia Hewitt!

Another deeper rumbling noise began to be heard, causing the walls and floor of the Main Hall to shake even more violently. Smashing sounds could be heard from the third floor: it was the Manor's roof. The building was collapsing!

The white light that held Adam continued to circle the room overhead, looking thicker in its density. I did not know what to do? The curator grabbed my arm and yelled for me to leave with him before it was too late. "My friend is in there" I shouted, pointing to the white, circling gloom. "You can't help him now", the curator pleaded.

A piece of the ceiling crashed down next to us and against my will I raced through the front door with the curator, trying not to look back. We made it outside the main entrance when I stopped running. "This is a mistake. I can't leave Adam in there", I cried and wrenched free from the curator's grasp that held me. I blindly dashed into the collapsing Main Hall. God, if ever there was a moment in my life that my heart beat as hard and as fast as it did then, I couldn't recall. Without thinking it through, with no reason to believe it would accomplish anything, I leapt through the air and into the glowing encumberment that held Adam.

Chapter IX

Then, it became so very quiet. I was on my feet and standing in Ringwood's second floor hallway, just outside the bedroom where Adam hid under the bed. The only light I could detect was coming from the gas lamps in the hall. The Manor was no longer in the throes of collapsing: the weeping and wailing voices were gone.

A few yards before me was the main staircase and I could see Adam a few steps down, just above the middle landing. He was looking into a mirror on the staircase wall. His look was one of exasperation and shock as he observed his image in the mirror. He had yet to notice me as I moved closer and soon I could see the reflection in the mirror WAS NOT ADAM. It wore the same Victorian suit that Adam was wearing but the face belonged to Abram Hewitt!

This was Adam's dream. I took a few steps closer, not sure if he could see me at all. I glanced past Adam when, inexplicably, she was there: Amelia Hewitt, standing at the bottom of the stairs, not hovering above the floor or surrounded in any glowing encasement of light, but as a young Amelia without death's shroud. Adam noticed her just then also.

"Silly goose! There you are. Come to dinner, father and the guests are waiting", Amelia said, and after a moment's hestitation Adam began descending the stairs towards her. My heart was racing, I knew that something was very wrong with this moment in time. I can't even speculate how I knew but I impulsively reacted to try and stop Adam, or this dream, or whatever it was, would never end.

"NO" I screamed, "Adam, you can't go with her". He turned, stunned by my presence, but it did not stop his slow descent down the stairs.

"Jason... wha... what the hell are you doing here? I don't understand. What is happening?"Adam's trembling voice spurted out. From behind him I heard Amelia again:

"Abram, why do you dally so? Father will be angry".

I was obvious she couldn't or wouldn't see me. Her words drew Adam's attention once again. I feared he would be totally oblivious of me if I didn't do something. He looked towards me again, letting me see the confusion in his face. The image in the mirror was no longer that of Abram Hewitt, there was no reflection at all.

"She loves me, Jason" he whispered.

"No, she doesn't, Adam. She does not know you. She only sees Abram Hewitt, not you. Something has happened here that has put us in this place and time where we don't belong. I don't know how or why, but if you go with her it will be the same dream continuously repeating. Adam, I know you can't understand what I'm trying to tell you now but you'll never get your true reality back unless you listen to me. Otherwise, this scenario, this moment will loop over and over again.

"If you stay, it will be an unfair and unjust love because you don't belong here. You'll have Abram Hewitt's body but not his soul. Amelia will never have the chance to love the real Abram Hewitt and she has to have that chance for things to be right. She deserves that chance. That's why she can't leave the Manor, Adam, because she's looking for Abram's soul to spend eternity with".

It was a moment of truth if ever there was one. Only the sound of the burning gas lamps could be heard. Adam kept his eyes on Amelia and I can't remember how much time passed or even if time moved at all. After what seemed like eons, Adam started up the stairs, heading for the bedroom where this entire saga began. "Abram, where are you going? Please, Abram, this is not like you" Amelia called out pleadingly. Adam halted short of entering the room and turned towards her: "It's all right, my dearest Amelia. Everything will be all right now".

How I knew what to do next could not be explained but instinctively I moved ahead of Adam into the bedroom. Something told me to keep a distance between us and give him room to pass. He silently ambled beyond where I stood, in a windowless corner at the opposite side of the bed. It was dark and we said nothing. After a few moments he knelt to the floor without so much as a glance in my direction, and slipped under the bed's frame, out of my view.

The room began to change. I could see the hallway gas lamps begin to fade away, morphing into the security lights that I was familiar with, and I noticed the security beam across the doorway again. The room returned to the musty, stale smell that the Manor adopted over the years. My heart was pounding, anxiety was overcoming me as I pondered how I was going to get out of here without being detected until a distant buzzing noise raced through my consciousness from some far away point. Within moments before me there was absolute black, a deep non-receding black as I have never seen before. Slowly I began to distinguish a small light near to my face. I strained for some recognition, some focus, when my eyes slowly adjusted to the contrast of light and black and I realized the light I saw came from the digital clock that rest on the table next to my bed at home.

It was 4:01 a.m.

Chapter X

By 6:00 a.m. I was sitting up on the edge of my bed. I could hear my automatic coffee-maker click on: a small blessing. I dragged myself to the sink with the hopes that some cold water on my face would remove the cobwebs I still felt entangling my brain. If all that was a dream, and only a dream, then why did my body ache so? And what the hell day was it that I set the alarm to wake me barely after the sun was up?

The calendar on my kitchen wall gave me the date: December 2nd, Sunday morning. My God, it's the day I'm supposed to pick Adam up after his overnight stay at Ringwood. Whether it was relief or disbelief I can't recall, but I remember sighing heavily and giving an out loud "damn" to no one but myself. Quickly, I gathered my things and headed out the door for the long ride to Ringwood.

This time Adam was not outside of the Manor when I got there. With trepidation I waited for the doors to open and as planned I straggled in with the first group of visitors. I stayed with them until they finished their viewing of the second floor and left. An ominous feeling was with me when I peered into the bedoom where (I hoped) Adam was hiding. "Hack, c'mon out now. All's clear" I called, trying to keep all this in perspective, my heart again beating rapidly until Adam came crawling out from under the bed, camera in one hand, flashlight in the other. He apparently just woke up, hurrying to my side in the hallway where I relieved him of his backpack.

"Hope you brought coffee, pal", Adam said, and I don't know if he ever understood why I was so very glad to hear him say that. With my arm on his shoulder I ushered him down the hall.

"It's on me, my friend. Anything you goddamn want, it's on me". He was puzzled by my exuberance.

Adam told me that nothing occurred last night during his Ringwood venture, nothing out of the ordinary. Here and there house sounds became a little frightening but he said his fear became boredom quickly and near to morning he fell asleep under the bed. We stopped for breakfast at a local diner, Adam had a hearty appetite I suspect partially because it was my treat. He was the friend I knew long ago, showing no trace that what I experienced was no more than my own nighttime imagery.

A week later Adam called me on the phone: "Jason, don't be angry, but next week Ringwood starts their Victorian Christmas tours and you know I'm part of it each year. Well…I sort of threw your hat in the ring this year because we were short of volunteers. I hope you'll do it with me buddy." There was a silence following this request and I know he was waiting for a reaction from me. "Listen", he began again, "if you don't want to do it, no big deal. I'll call them tomorrow".

I wondered if I sounded as flushed as I felt, maybe it was from embarassment or fear that I could feel my temperature rise. He seemed taken aback that I was taking this long to respond to what he conceived was a simple request. Finally, I ended the silence: "Oh, what the hell", I answered, "Let's go for it".

Epilogue

Our participation in the Manor's Victorian Christmas was uneventful, yet fulfilling to me because of what occurred: absolutely nothing. There were no ominous sounds, collapsing walls, ghostly spectres, all of what I attributed to an amazingly real and surreal dream. The weekend was flawless as visitor after visitor passed through Ringwood's grandeur.

The following spring Adam left; seeking someplace he probably knew didn't exist, in real Jack Kerouac style. I drove him again, this time to the Delaware Water Gap, a point where New Jersey and Pennsylvania meet, dissected by the Delaware River and connected by Route 80. His goodbye was short as he gathered his backpack. I watched from a nearby visitor's center parking lot as Adam hitched a ride from a van that stopped to pick him up. I was a cold and empty feeling I had as I watched him drive away. I think I returned home with somewhat of a broken heart.

From time-to-time I would receive a letter from Adam, each from a different locale throughout the country. He often wrote from towns I couldn't find on any map and his letters were mostly about the people he'd met and their vibrancy for life. Never a word about himself, even to my inquiries of his well-being that were in the letters I wrote to him.

In Shelby, Montana, Adam met a girl named Sarah. They got a small apartment together in town where Adam freelanced for a local newspaper and played a few nights with a group of local musicians, doing small gigs whenever they could.

That brings me back to the CD I'm listening to as I read Adam's latest letter. As I mentioned, it was a live performance that featured his flute playing, a haunting, lilting melody wafted from my speakers. The song returned again and again to a beautifully, enchanting phrase that was both stirring and provocative. Even though Adam wrote it was an original piece I could swear I've heard it before. As the music played I read the rest of Adam's letter that mentioned the title of the song.

Adam named it "For Amelia".

Ben Franklin's Dream

General Washington, presiding over the gatherings of these dignified and respected gentlemen assembled here in Philadelphia, couldn't help but grin when he noticed Ben Franklin sleeping in his seat. After all, the distinguished Mr. Franklin was in his 80's and had served his country above and beyond the call of an ordinary man. His list of servitude was long and extraordinary and he brought the maturity of his wisdom and experience to these endless, hot summer days where these men from the highest ranks of society pounded out the standards of what was to become the Constitution of the United States. Mr Franklin deserved to rest and not a man there disputed that fact, nor disturbed him in his slumber. Mr.Washington saw to that.

But Ben Franklin's rest was not an easy one. Age overtook his body, but left his mind intact, as sharp as it ever was, so while his body needed sleep, his visions were rampant. Only now they were framed with the memories of his life. In his sleep, he stood on the piers in Boston again, as he did as a young man when he yearned to be a sailor. He peered out at the distant horizon and imagined how it would be to journey across the water, beyond what he could see.

In his dreams, he saw himself working again for his demanding brother, James, knowing that he could do so much more on his own. He saw himself in the dark of the evening, slipping his writings underneath the door of his brother's newspaper shop so they would get published. It was a necessary task because James would never publish anything Ben wrote so Ben used a fictitious pen name: Poor Richard.

He relived the moment again that he left Boston for New York after James arrest for printing "scandalous libel" in his newpaper, The Courant, along with his own reluctance to keep afloat his brother's printing shop. Ben was wont to seek a destiny that he seemed driven for, but New York had all the printers it could use, so it was on to Philadelphia. Philadelphia welcomed him, and it was there that he met his sweet, beloved Deborah. She laughed at him as he walked through the streets carrying a loaf of bread under each arm, eating on a third as he walked along. "Methinks it strange to be so hungry as to carry your meal under your sleeves", she said, "if one is so hungry, then a proper respite would do nicely".

He was enamored immediately at her beauty and coyness. "If there were one such as you to enjoy these additional warm loaves with that I carry", Ben answered, "then a respite would be the order of the day". How wonderful to be here again with Deborah! He had forgotten how beautiful she was, her love was his inspiration to do great things. He stirred restlessly in his Convention chair.

"Mr. Franklin, sir, are you alright? Would you like a drink of water?" This aroused him to consciousness, and the mention of water gave him glimpses of his first journey to sea, to test his theory of the Gulf Stream, he called it. He was, he guessed, a sailor after all, but not in the fashion he yearned for as a lad. "Yes, thank you, kind sir", he responded and took the glass of water from Mr Madison. Always the gentlemen, Ben listened politely for a while to the ramblings of whoever had the floor, but the weariness of age soon put him back to deep rest.

His youth returned, and he saw the brave, young men who united with him to fight against the ravages of fires that destroyed people's homes and lives. Some called the place where they congregated a "firehouse", and it seemed like a good idea. Philadelphia kept it going, putting together more volunteers and more firehouses. Ben liked the idea of saving people's lives and property.

He saw the vision of himself in his Postmaster General's uniform made for him by Deborah, then the next moment he stood on the deck of a ship waving goodbye to her, sailing to France as a statesman. Wasn't it just a moment ago he was working so studiously on his "Poor Richard's Almanac" as its publisher? And what happened to the music of his Armonica? Its lilting, tuneful reverberations brought a smile of wonder to even Mozart and Beethoven. It was his proudest achievement.

How he panicked when his country began its fight for freedom from King George's tyranny. In his dreams he did what life did not allow him to do, he acted scared because war scared him. In real life it was expected of Ben Franklin to hold that composure and resolve he was well known for.

He cried in his sleep when he called to his son William in the distance, only to have the lad turn his back on him and walk away. That little boy he held above life itself, that same young man who held onto the kite in the storm to test his theory of electricity, decided his father was wrong in all he did and wanted no part of him. He pleaded through his tears that it was only in this dream that his sweet daughter Sarah and little boy Francis died and that in the waking world they lived on and prospered. For all his acumen in life, he was not a successful father, too busy to be close to those who needed him most. The pain of his broken heart translated to a mumbling heard by those at the Constitutional Convention. "How could anyone sleep in this oppressive heat?" wondered Thomas Mifflin allowed, but Ben continued to sleep.

He stood in a room with a single table. On the table were his creations, such as his monocles, his wood stove, his lightning rod, the keys to the Library of Philadelphia and even that curious candle he made from whale oil to avoid having a smoky laboratory.

Outside the room, he could hear people clapping and cheering for these items, but in this dream, unlike his reality, he was angry, and yelled that if he hadn't come up with these ideas, then someone else would have, that they were not so great as the people believed. The clapping and cheering stopped and his heart beat loudly in the silence. Great inventions, great ideas, he believed, were those creations that were unique to one man alone, that no other man could ever have conceived of. He lived in the frustration of believing that he never had an idea that approached such magnitude. His life raced by in his dreams and he saw all the things he didn't do that he should have done. For a man that has done more than any man before, he was still able to see the "what ifs" in his life.

"The floor needs Mr Franklin's vote on the matter before us", General Washington said loudly, stirring Ben Franklin to consciousness. He did not know the item being discussed that waited for his ballot, but he'd been here before. A glance at George for either a yea or a nay was all he needed. One wink meant a yea and that was what he saw.

"Yea, gentlemen, yea, yea and yea", he responded, and the room broke into laughter. The mirth of the moment was a welcome addition to the somberness and seriousness of the event.

Thank God for George, Mr Franklin thought, such a fine, upstanding young fellow. He lived in awe of General Washington's courage and insight into the human spirit, and what man better understood what makes another man conform to his duties. There was none better to sit at the head of these ceremonies. So different from, say, Mr Hancock, who each day make sure all knew he was in attendance.

Now, it had come to this. Ben Franklin was an old man in a new nation. He had seen many changes, and gave what he could for the benefit of his fellow man. He knew there was not a lot of time left. God, how he hoped his religious upbringing was accurate, and he could soon join his beloved Deborah who, after 44 years, left him alone in this world while he was in Paris. He never had the chance to say goodbye and that was the one thing now he truly wanted, that above all he ever did for anyone, was his hearts desire. You see, in his dreams, he cried at her loss everyday... but only in his dreams.

"We are done now, Ben" John Adams whispered, "the work of these many weeks must now be presented to the people".

"Just as well", Ben Franklin replied, "I find my own living room chairs much more comfortable for a man's rest than what we have here".

At 81, he still had work ahead, but Ben Franklin's dreams were the glimpses of his yearnings until he passed from this world at the age of 84.

The Mayor's Cow

Mama loved those long autumn Sunday drives. She would pile Aunt Mary and me into her little VW bug which was hard-pressed to carry even three people so I guess it was a good thing my brother Jim never wanted to go. Papa wasn't around much then. I remember that Papa's visits always made Mama cry, until she bought the VW and it became a new lease on life, an opportunity to escape I guess, and there we'd go motoring through the foothills of New Jersey.

I was no more than 8-years young, and that car's rear seat was my domain on those adventures. An honest admission is that I wasn't thrilled about the prospects of long, tedious hours spent chugging through unknown territory, often lost, hoping our car makes the next hill. I would rather have stayed home with my friends, or my dolls, sometimes even with James! But Mama felt secure with me nearby and I sensed even then the mother-daughter bonding that strengthened our love in the years to come.

Mama would choose a place to eat dinner as the destination of our quest. Usually a small restaurant located in some obscure New Jersey hamlet, named after a Native American tribe who lived in New Jersey long before anyone else did, or an American patriot deified in the fight for our country's liberty. Sometimes though, the eatery of our choice stood alone in the countryside, lost to even local folk who recalled the beanery we inquired about as legend, and no, they couldn't direct us to it, but maybe old Joe who owns the town's barber shop could help.

The Dutch Hill Inn was such a place. I still don't know how Mama was familiar with it, but she spoke of its quality and ambiance with great admiration. She and Aunt Mary were excited about this particular Sunday, so I gathered they'd been there before, maybe in some earlier life, with husbands behind the wheels and seemingly in command, smoking their pipes while they steered huge '55 Pontiacs that blanketed the width of the country lanes they drove them on.

Of course, locating the Dutch Hill Inn was a different matter. Its obscurity was of a great magnitude, entangled among the backwoods of Wayne, New Jersey, hiring daily because previous employees could not find their way back to work! We trudged up one road and down another, veering around sharp country curves, inquiring of roadside white-corn farmers peddling the labors of their lands if they even *heard* of our Dutch Hill Inn. All seemed hopeless until one fine gentleman acknowledged our query with a thoughtful skyward glance before he removed his pipe, and answered us with a very welcome and appreciated:

"Yep. Straight ahead, jest a few miles. Can't miss it."

We loved him. I sat now on the edge of my seat, staring with Mama and Aunt Mary out the front windshield, hungrily seeking a road sign, or even a mailbox telling us our famished journey had come to its close, when suddenly all of us spotted…her.

On our left, the land from the road ascended upward, grass-covered to its peak where a majestic white Victorian home sat on its crest. Racing down the hill at a speed here-to-fore unknown in the world of heifers, was a large black and white Jersey cow. She ran with purpose, with intent: to reach the other side of the road before we passed. Mama made a decision that fateful moment; not to be outdone by a half-ton cud-chewing dairy product. She introduced the Volkswagen's gas pedal to the floor.

We chugged mightily where now the road was flat, Mama cheering confidence that the race was won, but that cow saw it differently, and she surged ahead, reaching the road before we did until of all things in Heaven and Earth not to do: she froze. Smack dab in the middle of the asphalt she posed, unmoving, with an almost suicidal stare.

"Hold on, Joanie!" Mama yelled, both of her feet slamming clutch and brake, but woefully too late. I remember how quickly, how ominously huge the old cow became as we plowed headlong into her side, an impact that threw me forward, then backwards, all in a split-second. I could actually see the poor creature air-borne, head-over-tail bellowing her last hurrah as she landed on her back, with feet straight up, a ruin of blood and bruises.

After the impact we continued off the road on the opposite side, coming to a halt on a small downgrade. The three of us sat there numb until Mama became the first to collect her senses:

"Are you all-right, Joanie? Baby?" she asked anxiously as she sat me upright, her hands probing my head, arms and legs, and coming to rest as they gently cradled my face.

"I'm fine, Mama. Really." I assured her, but I noticed Aunt Mary still not moving, staring out the cracked front windshield:

"Do you think it's dead?" Aunt Mary asked, "it must be dead…I mean, we hit it so hard, and…"

"Mary" Mama answered calmly, "*we're* not dead. We can check the poor animal in a few moments."

The front of Mama's VW resembled a used bean-bag chair. The center of the hood crushed

downwards to the inside trunk's floor. Blood and animal waste covered the hood and I noticed the flies that wasted no time in locating a fresh meal. It was a time to be grateful the Volkswagen Corporation found it mechanically sound to put their car's engine in the rear trunk.

Save for the gurgling noises of life oozing from the body of our unfortunate victim, all was quiet.

Mama told me to run to the house on the hill, tell them what happened, that we've accidentally hit their cow and maybe they should come shoot it, or call the police, or something. "My cow?" the kindly farmer queried as he surveyed the situation on the road from his porch, "that ain't my cow, young lady.

That there's old Betsy-Lou, Mayor Jones' cow. She must've wandered off again...but it don't look like she'll be wandering back, do it?" he chuckled. Then he told me sure, he'll call the police and I best be getting back down the hill to Mama.

"The Mayor's cow!" I thought, "We'll be taken off to jail for sure" and I think my eyes were getting misty when I told Mama what I knew. She smiled ever so lightly, picking me up into her arms knowing I was frightened with this whole episode.

"The Mayor's cow, huh Joanie? Guess I'll have to offer to pay for her. How much do you think a cow cost?"

"Gosh, Mama, pay for a cow?" the idea was bewildering to me, "I'll bet she cost a million dollars! A million-trillion dollars!" Aunt Mary, always a serious woman, told me to not be so silly, that it was only a cow.

"Well, Joanie," Mama replied, "maybe to somebody she was worth a million-trillion dollars."

What followed is sparse in my memory: two police officers arrived, one who had the reluctant task of putting poor old Betsy-Lou out of her misery. The other officer found the situation very humorous, and though he tried valiantly not to, he eventually succumbed to laughter.

Mama's VW still ran. We looked pathetic, like a float in a Halloween parade, but it got us where we wanted to go. Where? The Dutch Hill Inn, of course. It was there, just a mile further down the road and it turned out to be a nice place. I don't remember exactly what we ordered, but I remember it wasn't steak. Mama, Aunt Mary and me enjoyed a good side-splitting laugh that must've been there hiding behind the tensions of the day's events.

"The mayor's cow, mama!" I said through my tears, "I can't believe we hit the mayor's cow".

Mama leaned over and whispered: "Joanie," she said, "thank goodness we didn't hit the Governor's cow!", and mama and I enjoyed our own private chuckle on that very special Sunday.

The Maestro's Gift

Centuries ago, nomads settled at the feet of the North Hills. They were attracted by it's serene settings and it's easily accessible location to the main trail that dissected the mountains promenades that stood as a barrier to the east. They surrendered their nomadic life alongside the Baasi River when they realized that here game was plentiful and the ground fertile. Generations after generations became farmers, growing all they needed and more. What they didn't need, the mountain's pass allowed them to develop commerce and trade their goods with other settlements for those items which they didn't have. As with their own settlement, all of their neighbor's homesteads grew into villages or towns. What these nomads eventually called home was given the name of Capaldi, a name that only their founding fathers knew the origin of but sadly took that knowledge to their great reward.

Their small village lie nestled at the foot of the North Hills. The nomads and their descendants found life in Capaldi very sustainable, agreeable as a place to raise their children and live in peace among themselves and their neighbors. Springs and summers of uncommon beauty, when the rolling hills and nearby forest glades bustling with the greenery of life that followed the harsh winters was when they felt truly blessed. Farms stretched from the south and west for many miles, built along the Baasi and using the river to water their crops and their livestock. Their bounty was plentiful, for what they took to market was always hearty in volume and more than enough to nourish the village and all nearby residents.

Capaldi also developed as a bustling village, it's village green becoming the center of Capaldians social life where they gathered for the celebration of the year's harvest, or their springtime festival, where their children could run and play while the adults discussed the latest news that came from beyond the North Hills. Capaldi thrived, and as with all developing communities, there were those that experienced a heartier bounty of goods as compared to their less fortunate brethren. But still it was a community of unity among its citizens, overseen by a small group of people that formed it's government. From its origins of tribal councils, through oligarchies and monarchies, Capaldi eventually adapted, through the insistencies of its people, to somewhat of a republic, with tinges of a democracy cradled in its doctrines. Town fathers, overseen by Mayor Sven, instituted the political and social mandates of Capaldi's citizenry.

The Molshoi Orchestra was the country's pride and joy, renowned throughout the world, having performed before royalty and heads-of-state, they were noted principally for not only their exquisite performances but also for their relentless schedule of touring, a demanding and grinding schedule that had them, year after year, present their music to the kings and queens of the world. They were led by the famous maestro Oleg Boriesky, the world's most accomplished violinist. Boriesky ruled with the perfection demanded by a man in his position, settling for nothing less than the absolute best from his orchestra members. The results were always the production of the most beautiful music any who heard them would agree upon. To attend a concert given by the Molshoi was a matter of decreed prestige since attendance was by invitation only. In general, only royalty and the upper class were privileged enough to savor the magnificence of Boriesky's troupe.

Late one summer word had reached the village of Capaldi that the Molshoi Orchestra had chosen Capaldi's village square as a rehearsal sight in preparing to perform before the Duke in the city of Aakbuur. Maestro Oleg Boriesky deemed it a convenient and strategic location to review the repertoire that would be offered to the Duke and his family. It wasn't a common practice, to rehearse in a public place among the common folk, but occasionally it was done if convenience presented itself. At a meeting of the town fathers, Mayor Sven read aloud the letter requesting lodging for the Maestro and his wife, Zocia, along with the members of his orchestra. The letter slated their arrival for early October. "It will not be too cold yet", remarked Mayor Sven to Capaldi's gathered village officials, "and they have requested the village square for their rehearsals, if that is possible. Our preparations will include a large, open-air tent in the square for their use. Oleg Boriesky had indicated that a preliminary performance for the orchestra under the stars in the brisk, autumn air would do them good, and it will be their way of thanking us for our expected hospitality. Oh! The people will come from miles around to hear such grand music!" Mayor Sven was clearly excited, he jittered nervously on the podium, his short, rotund frame bouncing in time with his pronounced exhortation. "There will be just enough time for us to arrange the accomodations. We must begin at once!"

"Most certainly," an exuberant widow Hansen replied, "I will meet with the ladies knitting club this evening to discuss arrangements. We will have the village newspaper announce the exciting news in tomorrow's paper." The widow Hansen was a tall, stately woman, given to nothing but an astute and impeccably dressed figure, especially since she was chosen to sit in the village council. She had been a widow for so long that there was hardly a man in the village who remembered a Mr. Hansen.

"Imagine! The great conductor Oleg Boriesky coming here to our little village!" she exclaimed excitedly. "We must prepare for this event. We must let him know he is so very welcome. Our appreciation should be expressed with gifts to the Maestro, of course!"

Boris Kneedle owned the village newspaper, *The Capaldi Word*. His great-grandfather started it when he himself was a young man, and it had been passed down to every Kneedle man since. Except, Boris never married, has no children and he is no longer a young man, so many of the townspeople wonder who will run the paper when Boris no longer can. "How thrilling this is", Boris Kneedle interjected, "that of all the places the Molshoi could have chosen, they have decided that our little village will be so honored".

The widow Hansen scampered out the door after the meeting's adjournment to begin the preparations. Mayor Sven and his assistants gathered together to discuss how they would reply to Oleg Boriesky, and what their first course of action should be after that. Boris Kneedle began jotting notes onto a small pad. Tomorrow, his newspaper would carry the great news to all the people of Capaldi and the nearby towns and villages.

"Hmph! Another village of peasants I have to be among in order that the world might hear my music," complained Oleg Boriesky angrily. He crumpled the letter from Mayor Sven that said the village of Capaldi graciously accepts the Maestro's terms and welcomes the Molshoi as their guests. "Why must I do this? These people will grovel before me, humbling themselves for a simple acknowledgement from me. I will be presented with their meager offerings, gifts of which I will have no use for. Then…"

"Oleg!" his wife Zocia brashly interrupted, "honesty, you are becoming more and more bitter in your old age. Who do you prattle so? You are of the same stock as these people. Were you not raised in a small village near Warsaw yourself? This village will be honored by your presence. Is not your respect at least the courtesy they deserve?"

"Respect? Bah!" Oleg Boriesky resounded harshly, "Zocia, when I was a young man I found music to be the true voice of Heaven, the calling of angels. I never thought of it as a sideshow, or a parade, or even an opportunity for fame. When I played, I played for the love of music, with all my heart and soul. Now, it is nothing more than to grandstand before kings and queens and dukes. Even the musicians in my orchestra…they can only read the notes on the pages before them. They do not hear what the music is saying, cannot feel it's pulse in their hearts, and my musicians are among the world's finest…" . He paused here, his anxiety eased him into his favorite chair by the window. "I grow weary, Zocia", he said softly, "I miss the time when it all meant something."

Zocia Boriesky had seen her husband like this before, but these moments of despair and bitterness were more frequent now. Maybe it was time he thought of retiring, but what would he do? Performing was all Oleg had ever known. She remembers when he loved it so, when it was all he ever lived for. It was why she fell in love with him, seeing him perform with the orchestra as a young man, the youngest violinist ever in Molshoi's history to be seated as first chair. The Molshoi had come to Zocia's little town where she met Oleg at the Grand Hall, being introduced to him by a common friend. How handsome he was! And so full of passion for his music, so intent in his belief that music belongs to the people and someday he would endure all would have the opportunity to hear this great orchestra…but that was a long time ago. This anger, particularly when it is directed towards people that offer their hospitality at the villages he chooses for the Molshoi rehearsals, is a sad thing. These people would otherwise never have heard Oleg perform. Has he forgotten how important that was to him once? Maybe now. Zocia thinks again, it is time for Oleg to stay home. "Oleg…", she whispers softly.

"I know, my dearest," he replies to her as yet unasked question, "it is time. I will announce to the world…that this upcoming performances before the Duke will be Oleg Boriesky's last. It has been a long time coming. I can no longer hold onto this dream that the magic in music, that beautiful aura I once basked in, will someday return. I prayed that if I traveled far and wide, and played in the towns and villages outside the cities, I would rediscover the heart and soul, that which is lost, in music. I hoped it dwelled among the people who live the way I once did, back when the music was alive. Alas, it is gone, my love." Zocia wiped away the tears on her face, turning her back so her husband could not see. Oleg smiled at her, but it was a sad smile. After so many years of marriage he still found it amazing he remained the object of this beautiful woman's love and devotion.

Hans Gilbert was only twelve years young and already he was losing his baby-face looks. He was beginning to show signs of having the chiseled, handsome features that his father had. Like his father, Hans was a farmer, not because he wanted to be, but because it was necessary. It was only he and his mother living on this great big piece of land, and the man's work was left up to him. She made sure his schooling was tended to, but in order for them to survive, the land and the animals had to be maintained.

Papa died when Hans was only nine. He remembers his father being sick for a long time with that bad cough, and always being very weak near the end. Still, papa did his best to keep up with his adventurous, young son. When the work was done, there was fishing and hunting and hiking and just running to do, but Hans remembers how papa lagged behind when he became ill. Papa loved to work with his hands. He was always making something from scraps of wood, toys for Hans and things mama could always use around their home. Papa made sure that Hans was always nearby, showing him the finer points of working with chisels, hammers and saws and all kinds of tools he kept in his workshop in the barn. His father was so happy when they were together, and when he wasn't coughing, or gasping for breathe, he was telling Hans about the world. Sometimes Hans would find his father staring at him and smiling, with tears in his eyes. Papa would quickly turn away. "I think the wind blew something into my eyes", he would say. Hans never knew that it was anything different than what papa said it was.

As time when on, papa became so weak. It was hard to see him lying in bed, not able to move so well or breathe without difficulty. "You'll be the man in the family, Hans", his father told him one day, "I'm just too tired anymore. Seems like the good Lord needs me to tend his fields and fix whatever is broken up there. But that's okay…it's good, honest work, son". Papa always had a way of putting things, different from mama, but Hans understood the meaning of these times. Knew his papa was the kind of sick that never gets better. "Just wish I could have hung around to see you grow, boy. I can tell you'll be a fine, young man. Now help me up, Hans. You and me need to go and sit on the back porch so I can show you something." Hans remembers mama being so upset to see papa so weak and trying to get out of bed, she expressed her disapproval, said he needed his rest, but also knew there was no way of stopping him. She wrapped a blanket around him and helped him into his slippers, then carefully supported him out the back door and onto a porch seat. Papa sat there for a long time saying nothing, wheezing and coughing into his handkerchief. After a few moments, he spoke to Hans: "It is a beautiful October evening, isn't it Hans? The sky is as clear as I have ever seen it". In Hans memory of that moment, a miracle, or omen occurred as both he and papa observed a shooting star racing across the sky, both marveling at its glory as it blazed into infinity.

"God always has a plan", papa said, "I know you can't understand this now, but I guess you need to see that my part of His plan on this good earth is finished.". Hans tears began to flow, he tried so hard for so long to be as brave as his papa wanted him to be but a boy at nine needs to cry sometimes. "Now Hans, you must be strong. No crying, there will be plenty of time for that later. I have something to show you." With that papa reached under the chair and pulled up a burlap sack. In the sack was a smooth wooden object, maybe a foot long and shaped a bit like mama's hourglass she got from her mama. It had a long wooden stem, or handle, attached. Hans had never seen anything like it before. "I don't have anything to leave you, Hans", his father said, "except this."

"What is it, papa?" Hans asked inquisitively.

"It was going to be a violin." papa answered, "Your mama and me wanted you to have some of the better things in life. When I was a boy I played the violin, but only for a short time. We were poor and my papa had to sell it to feed our family. I loved to play so much and cried very hard when your grandpa took it away forever. Mama and me can't afford a violin either, but I remember how mine felt when I held it how it balanced so beautifully in my arms under my chin. I was sure i could make you one just as magnificent, but there isn't going to be enough time…". Papa stopped to gather his strength. he coughed again into his handkerchief, then sat back in the chair, closing his eyes. Hans took the unfinished violin from his hands. It was marvelous. The wood was so pristine and fragrant: he had never run his hand over wood so smooth. How did papa do it, he thought?

"I planned on finishing it." Hans was startled by his papa being awake, "I…I am sorry, Hans, but I wanted you to have it anyway."

Hans held his father's gaze for a moment, then looked to the object in his hands, continuing to run his fingers over the hourglass-shaped wood. "I'll finish it, papa. I promise, I'll finish it for you and it will be the best violin anyone ever had! Then I'll grow up to be the best violin player in the whole world!"

"Good for you, son", his weakend father responded through moist eyes. "I knew I could count on you. Remember this night always, hold it in your heart, and your violin will play the music of the angels."

"I promise, papa. I promise".

Hans' father passed away later that same evening. He seemed content as Hans and his mama sat with each other at this bedside. They each held a hand as he closed his eyes for the last time. Hans cried and called for his papa all night. His uncle and neighbor came to carry papa to the place where he was to be buried, at the edge of their property, up on the hill where he could always see the night sky so clearly.

Hans worked on his father's violin whenever he could. He wasn't the craftsman that papa was yet, but he remembered so much of what his father taught him. Papa left sketchings for Hans, and he borrowed books from school about music that had pictures of violins in them.

His mother found a violin teacher in Vernskot, a small town about twelve miles north, and she took Hans there once a week. His music teacher, Mr Carlotta, accepted eggs and milk and a basket of corn or tomatoes, or whatever Hans' mama could bring as payment for his lessons. Hans's violin hadn't been completed yet, it needed only strings which they couldn't afford, so Hans learned to play on his teacher's instrument, but he wasn't allowed to take it home. Hans was an eager student and was learning fast, but he needed to practice, so Mr Carlotta bought a set of strings for Hans' violin. "You'll pay me back someday, Hans," Mr Carlotta told him, "but you play beautifully and need to have your own instrument at home to practice on".

When Hans brought his violin to Mr Carlotta so he could put the new strings on, his teacher was speechless at the beauty of Hans' work. The violin glistened a deep, textured brown, with a magnificent etching on its back of a stream cascading through a forest glen, framed by rising hills in the distance. it's tone was flawless, each pluck of the bow, each vibrato, every trill was perfect in its resonance.

"Hans, how could you have made such a beautiful violin before you even knew how to play?" Mr Carlotta asked.

"It was my father's work," Hans replied, "all I did was finish what he began."

From that day forth, Mr Carlotta taught Hans with a zest reserved for only his most promising students, but fate played another hand. After just a little more than a year of taking lessons, Hans and his mama showed up on a Saturday morning as usual for Hans' lesson but Mr Carlotta's house was empty and locked. A neighbor came from across the street and gave them a package and a letter addressed to Hans. It was from Mr Carlotta. Seems his sister has beome very ill and needs help. She lives too far away to travel back and forth so Mr Carlotta found it necessary to pack up his belongings and move in with her and her children. "I hope to see you again someday," he wrote in his letter to Hans. "Never stop playing. Your music is your soul and you express it wonderfully. You will find I have left for you some music books that should help you. I will never forget you, Hans." And just like that, Mr Carlotta was gone from Hans' life.

His determination to play was stronger than ever now, though his mother wondered how he would be able to continue without a teacher. Hans practiced everyday whenever he could. He never neglected his duties of tending to the farm, so he was up before the sunrise practicing Beethoven and Mozart in the barn, and playing Chopn and Verdi at the day's end in his room. He played and played whenever he could. His mama was proud, but concerned that her eleven-year old little boy did not have that many friends and neglected things that eleven-year old boys should be doing.

"Don't worry, mama," Hans would tell her, "I'm doing what papa wanted me to do. I play because I must, it is a part of me, a magic! I believe that papa felt that same magic when he was a young man playing his violin."

One day, mama came to Hans with the news about the Maestro coming to Capaldi. "Isn't it exciting?" she exclaimed. "The Molshoi Orchestra will be performing for us. Mayor Sven has asked that we offer what we can to honor them: a gift of food or a place to stay. We have no room here in our little cottage but I can give them eggs and vegetables while they are here in town. The mayor says it is our village tradition that each of us give something.

"May I give them something also, mama?" Hans asked.

"Of course, Hans. We will go to the village the night of their performance and sit with the others. Why, I remember your papa speaking so highly of Maestro Boriesky and his music."

"But what should I give as a gift, mama?"

"Hans, I am sure you will think of something. Maybe you can give him one of your beautiful carvings?" mama replied. "Dear Hans, we cannot give a gift as expensive as Mrs Hansen's, but I am sure that Maestro Boriesky will be pleased with any offering we make."

"Yes, mama," a disappointed Hans replied, but inside he was afraid of looking foolish to the rest of the village. What would papa do, he wondered? "May I be excused?" Hans suddenly said.

"Certainly Hans", mama answered, "aren't you feeling well?"

"Yes, mama, I feel find. I will have a better appetite tomorrow." With that said, Hans scurried out the back door. Mama smiled at her little boy becoming so much the man her husband was, yet still having so much of that little boy left inside.

Wilfreda Hansen was determined to let the world know of her intentions, and that was very typical of her, especially if it meant doing something most others could not afford to do. She held the golden bow gently in her hands, displaying it for the men in the room to see.

"Isn't it beautiful?" she boasted. Mayor Sven looked at the bow with an air of indifference. He was used to the widows' tactics and bragging mannerisms. "Yes, widow Hansen, it is quite the offering. I am sure Oleg Boriesky will be thrilled. Now, if we could continue with the arrangements for the band shell," and with that all talk of gifts and offerings were set aside so they might complete their plans for the upcoming Molshoi performance.

October tenth was the day the Molshoi was scheduled to arrive and the train station was packed with eager villagers waiting in anticipation. When the trains did arrive and Oleg Boriesky appeared in the train's doorway, the crowd cheered and the small village band played. Mayor Sven nervously stood at the forefront on the station's platform. Alongside him were the widow Hansen, her son William, and the other leading citizens of Capaldi.

The Mayor stepped forward and as the crowd became silent, he held aloft the paper that contained the short speech he had written for this occasion: "Maestro Borieky, Madame Boriesky, and to all the members of your wonderful Molshoi Orchestra, as the mayor of Capaldi and speaking on behalf of all of its citizens, we wish to welcome you to our little village. We are truly honored by your presence.

"We are hoping your stay with us will be a most memorable one as you prepare for your performance before the Duke. It is our intention to accomodate your every need. Welcome! One and all!", and with that the crowd cheered heartily while the band played once again. Mayor Sven held up his hands: "Silence, please" he pleaded to the gather ing, "let the Maestro speak."

Oleg Boriesky said nothing, standing there in uncomfortable silence for what seemed entirely too long for such an occasion. He scanned the crowd from face-to-face, appearing both restless and discommoded, even disturbed. The tone of his voice when he finally did speak was the tone of a man who appeared bothered by the situation he was in.

"Yes...well, Mr Mayor, I am ill adjusted these days to the pomp-and-circumstance you have so pain stakingly arranged for our arrival. We are grateful, but if you would please excuse my wife and I and see us to our quarters. it has been a long journey and there are tedious days of preparation that lie ahead. Thank you and the good citizens of...Capaldi." His mentioning the village by name was hesitant, almost as if he had to take a moment to recollect where he was.

With that said, Oleg Boriesky left the train platform, trailed close behind by his wife Zocia who seemed embarrassed by her husband's abruptness and slight. The widow Hansed was even without words for just a few moments, but she quickly recouped and bounded forward to take Maestro Boriesky's arm. "Maestro, you will be staying with me. My name is Wilfreda Hansen and I have the finest and most grand of all the houses here in Capaldi. I am sure you will be pleased."

"Madam," Boriesky replied, "if you have also the most comfortable bed for our stay, then I will be surely impressed. If you would please have someone take our bags."

"William!" the widow called to her son, "take Mr and Mrs Boriesky's bags to our home at once." She turned her attention again to Boriesky: "Maestro, I know you are anxious to get settled, but my son William so wanted to meet you. He plays the cello and has been tutored by the finest teachers from the city, and how he worships you! Isn't that right, William? William?" but William Hansen was nowhere to be found. He managed to find the company of a young lady traveling with the orchestra and as young men are wont to do, he forgot his mother's demands and instructions, choosing instead to accompany the young lady to the place where she was residing, carrying her luggage for her. The Boresky's bags remained on the station's platform.

"Well, madam," Oleg Boriesky addressed the widow Hansen, "it seems that I am a fallen idol and you will be our page. if you don't mind, we are quite tired and wish to rest." He and Zocia stepped into the waiting coach and signaled the coachman to depart, leaving the widow and his luggage behind. A humbled and angry Widow Hansen gathered the Boriesky's bags, stuggling under their weight. "William!" she shouted over and over as she began the arduous task of transporting the luggage to her home.

Zocia Boriesky was reeling from her husband's most impolite departure from the welcoming prepared for him. She said nothing during the ceremonies, as she was wont to do, but soon could hold her silence no longer. "My husband," she began, "you have never been anything but cordial to those who admire you. Why have you chosen to shun these fine people? I dread to think what light they hold you in now." Oleg Boriesky offered no excuse or response. He stared blankly out the coach window at the passing landscape with its small homes and farms.

"This village and the countryside" he finally offered, "is so very much like the place where I lived as a young man before I left for Venice. It reminds me of how life was with father after mother died. We had no other family, only him and I, but we managed.

"How he loved his music! It made him very happy and it was from him that I learned to play. When he could teach me no further he sent me away. I never could account for how he was able to afford it. Zocia, with all I have done - the symphonies, the concerts, and leading the Molshoi to perform before royalty and the cheers of a thousand people - nothing has ever rang true in my heart as when I played for my papa in our home. It is that magic I miss so very much.

"I played for him on my first violin, which he made himself with his very own hands. Ah, Zocia…what a sweet instrument it was! In all my years I have never played another like it. It's sweet timbre would glide very so ever so softly, filling the air with the music of angels. My papa would cry when I played for him. I would ask him why there were tears in his eyes and he would never answer."

Oleg Boriesky became silent after that, Zocia have never heard her husband in the throes of emotion such as this. He had not talked before of his family, she met Oleg after his father passed and she made the decision long ago that if he did not speak of it, she would never ask. Except for now, just one question: "What became of that violin, my husband?". Her inquiry was almost apologetic.

Oleg did not remove his gaze from the world outside the coach window. His reply was sullen.

"There was a fire…I was away. They say papa fell asleep with his pipe still lit. Everything. My papa, the violing, our little house…all was lost. Now even the village itself I understand is gone. Hard times had befallen, I assume."

"I am sorry, my dearest husband. I did not know…".

"No need, my dear", he responded, "it is I who seeks repentance and ask for your foregiveness for not having told you this so long ago, but I did not allow it into my memory until this visit." The coach came to a halt and the coachman stepped down to open the carriage door. "Zocia, my papa cried when he heard me play. It was music from a violin not made in Vienna or by any European craftsman, but made by him with his own love. I had so many questions for him but papa died before I had the chance. What made him cry when I played? Alas, I will never know. This had laid heavily on my soul lately, and nowadays when I am conducting before an audience I can only see these people hearing the music but not understanding its depth, its meaning. I have come to realize I have spent much of my life searching for someone who can be so moved by the music as my papa was."

"Tired? Nonsense! The man was downright rude, I say!" barked the police chief Peter Ivank. He was angry about the brusque manner that Oleg Boriesky excused himself from the crowd gathered at the train station. "He didn't give two shakes about our welcome. Furthermore, a man of that character is not worthy of our gifts." Mayor Sven saw the task before him, attempting to soothe the tempers of this meeting of the town officials. But maybe their anger is justified? After all, it was a bewidered crowd that left the station afer Boriesky's unexpected departure, and it was all he could do to calm the pending storm. He quickly explained to the throng gathered that day that the Maestro had a long and arduous journey, and he needed immediate rest inorder to guarantee an astute performance at tomorrow's rehearsal. "Now, Peter," Mayor Sven directed to the chief, "Maesto Boriesky is still a guest to our village and I am sure all will be well this evening. He was sent notice all are welcome to attend the Moshoi's rehearsal, and certainly we cannot dictate to our people whether or not the Maesto is worthy of their gifts. I would rather it be the villagers personal decision."

"Well…I, for one, feel is is our duty to present our offerings", the Widow Hansen reiterated, "and as you know I have a very fine gift for the Maestro, especially after I had the good fortune to meet him and his lovely wife at the train station. Why, he told me he would even be willing to hear my William perform!"

"Fine. Yes, Mrs Hansen," Mayor Sven interrupted, and as with everyone else in the room that wasn't quite the recall they had of the Widow Hansen's encounter with Oleg Boriesky, "that is all fine. Now if we can adjourn and retire to our homes in preparation for this evening. We will meet at the rehearsal tent at 7:00 sharp." Mayor Sven concluded the meeting before the Widow

Hansen could continue with the braggadocio for which she has become well known.

The ride to Capaldi for Hans and his mother was never too long a ride. Their old mare's leisurely pace through the countryside into town was a precious time for the two of them. It was here that Hans learned much about life from his mother as she told him stories of her life and her father's, stories from the Bible, and just pearls of wisdom that Hans relished forever. They traveled through the small valley, surrounded by the beautiful, snow-capped mountains of the North Hills, through lush fields of hay and corn, past fields and farms. Hans noticed every vista, was aware of every scent, felt every ray of sunshine that touched his face.

Nellie Gilbert held a small box that contained several bottles of homemade perserves on her lap; it was their gift to Maestro Boriesky. Hans kept a steady grip on the reigns, though he didn't really have to. Their old horse knew the way to Capalid with or without riders, but Hans loved to pretend he was driving a fine royal carriage pulled by a team of the King's mighty horses. He would make his grand entrance tonight at the concert in full regalia, escorting the princess to tonight's performance. In fact, the tent for the concert was on this very same road. "Make way for the princess," he imagined he would shout as the crowd parted and cheered. "Mother, I thought this night would never come," Hans said. "I am nervous when I think of presenting our gifts to the Maestro. What should I say? Should I bow?"

"You'll do fine, Hans," his mother replied in a soothing and reassuring tone, "just be yourself. I will be with you." Hans always trusted his mother's words, she was so wise and he was so very proud of her. He noticed how pretty she looked this evening in her finest pink dress with the pink ribbon in her hair to match. He noticed how she could still turn men's heads whenever they went into town and didn't know if that made him angry or pleased.

Soon the tent came into their view. It was a huge, open gray tent that covered a large part of the field where it was put up. Hans thought it reminded him of the tent the circus used when they were here last summer. As they pulled their carriage into the clearing, Hans could see the musicians on the stage mulling about, shuffling papers and removing their instruments from cases. There was the sound of several instruments playing in a discordant noise, tuning, Hans supposed. It grew louder as more of the musicians took their seats. He could not see the Maestro anywhere but imagined he would be along soon. Quite a few of the villagers, along with some folks from nearby towns, were there already. Some benches were provided but most chose to either stand, or sit on blankets they brought along and spread on the grass. Hans saw some of his classmates scurrying about. It was a perfect Autumn evening as he and his mother seated themselves on a bench in the very first row. "So close to the stage, mama. This is wonderful!"Hans marveled. As the sun sank lower in the sky on this fall day, Hans noticed the sweet aroma of the season. The smell of burning pine from several fires outside the great tent saturated the air; it was the blending of the firewood's aroma and the comfortable coolness of the dusk of this day that brought back the memories of Han's father to him. He loved this time of year and near the end of his life found an inner peace that he should die when the leaves were golden brown on the trees and the birds were venturing overhead to their winter havens. "Mother, if you'll excuse me, I need to get something from the carriage."

"Of course, Hans,"she replied, "but hurry back before the Maestro takes his place on the stage."

"Yes, mother," Hans answered and hurried off. At the carriage Hans reached underneath the seat and pulled out a long box. He held it closely and looked skyward, noticing for the first time in a while how many stars glistened overhead. At that very moment a shooting star burned quickly across the Heavens, displaying a life of a brilliant, narrow fire that sparkled in its glory and within a blink of an eye was lost forever except to those like Hans who were witness to its brief but monumental existence. "I understand, father," Hans whispered softly to himself, then quickly returned to this mother's side. She noticed the box he now carried but said nothing. She knew that if it was important enough for Hans to bring, then he would, in his own time, show her what it was.

The excitement of the event was vivid in the air in anticipation of the concert. The gathering crowd forgot any indignation they might have harbored earlier as soon as Maestro Boriesky appeared on the stage. As he spoke to the musicians near him, Mayor Sven also took the stage and addressed the crowd: "Good citizens of Capaldi and our neighbors," he boomed loudly, "our village is deeply honored to host the most celebrated and distinquished Molshoi Orchestra, under the direction of the great Maestro Oleg Boriesky." The crowd displayed its approval with applause, Mayor Sven waved his hands, palms down, in a gesture requesting silence so he might continue his speech. "This is the Molshoi's final rehearsal prior to their command performance before the Duke. It is my pleasure to introduce our principal guest and conductor, the most illustrious Maestro Boriesky."

Polite applause greeted the Maestro as he stepped atop his small podium on stage. Certainly not the thunderous greeting that some anticipated. One could only imagine that the cold shoulder he gave his welcoming committee at the train station carried some lingering effects after all. Boriesky shuddered at this introduction, and if not from a plea by Zocia would not have tolerated it. She insisted on his cordiality, reminding him that this was the Mayor's chance at a brief moment of prestige and any honorable guest would respect that. He took a polite bow before the audience, then turned towards his orchestra, baton raised in his right-hand. He knew that his demand for their readiness was never compromised at these moments.

Hans was one of the few who clapped heartily when the Maestro took the stage. He had not been at the train station when Oleg Boriesky arrived, but even so, what do young boys know of such mattters, of politics and such affairs? He saw beyond that and applauded loudly with the exuberance and expectation of the night's offerings.

The music began. The soft, low overtones of Mendelsohn embraced the evening air. Hans became enraptured, his heart beat faster with the allegro of Mozart, his eyes moistened with the sad, emotional expressions of Brahms. He sat on the edge of his seat, exhilarated by the strident reflections of Beethoven. He never imagine that music could be as invigorating to one's spirit as the sound of Bach journeyed outward from the stage, out into eternity. Hans was aware of Maestro Boriesky's perfection. Because this concert was a rehearsal, he carefully observed the Maestro's emphasis of several fine points between each piecce, addressing an individual musician or an entire section on stage. He never seemed satisfied at the end of any one number, but Hans imagined it was this way with all men of such regal platitudes. Often, the Maestro raised his hands in disgust, simply motioning for the musicians to continue without any particular direction from him. He was a stern taskmaster, not even satisfied with his performance on the violin of an etude by Chopin that Hans thought was brilliant, but he noticed Boriesky's look of disgust at its conclusion, holding his instrument an arm's length from him with an appearance of disdain and displeasure.

At the rehearsal's conclusion the crowd warmed to Oleg Boriesky and the Molshoi's spectacular performance. The ovation had the people standing as Boriesky took his traditional bow, and signaled to his first chair musicians to do the same. Again, Mayor Sven came to center stage and waved his arms asking for the crowd's silence. He congratulated the Maestro and the entire Molshoi Orchestra on such a splendid performance, thanking them repeatedly for such a spectacular night of music on Capaldi's village green. The mayor then announced it was time to present to the Maestro, as is customary, gifts from the citizens of Capaldi in appreciation. An obviously disgruntled Oleg Boriesky sat on the end of the stage as one-by-one he accepted the villager's gifts. Zocia sat nearby, reminding him with her deliberate gaze that he must honor these people with a dignified air. Boriesky was wont to notice her at every turn.

The villager's came forth. Boriesky graciously acknowledged their offerings with a nod, or a small compliment. The Widow Hansen presented her gift, a beautiful Rosewood baton with gold inlays. She beamed proudly, and obviously intended to draw the attention of those near enough to hear her. "Oh Maestro," she began, "I've been told this baton is the only one of it's kind in the city. That's where I had to purchase it, you see. The finest European tradesman crafted it, possibly you've heard of him? Now, what was his name? Just a moment, I believe I can recollect it if…".

Blah, blah, blah, blah was all Boriesky could hear. The loving devotion of his wife and her demands on his character were being teted with this pompous windbag rattling before him. "Ah, yes, madam…" he interrupted her, "I must say your gift is quite… extravagant is the word I seek. I am almost embarassed by it; it is much too nice a baton to ever be waved so vigorously on stage. I will keep it in its case, resplendent of its fine detail to remain untarnished for all to see. Now, tell me, how is your son? You mentioned earler today how much an admirer of mine he is." A startled Widow Hansen found herself taken aback by the Maestro's straight-forwardness, not really able to grasp if he was appreciative of her gift, or he was embellishing an indignity upon her with sarcasm.

"Why...yes, he's right here..." She turned to her side where William was just moments ago, but that was moments long gone. "WILLIAM," she screamed, "where are you? WILL...".

"Madam," Boriesky again interrupted her, "if my power of recall is correct, and my memory of your son as the young man with the penchant for young ladies is accurate, then I believe I can see him out there by the carriages, engrossed in conversation with one of the young ladies of your village. It would seem the ardor of me has again taken a back seat to the callings of his puberty." The Widow Hansen excused herself politely and stormed away towards her son. Oleg Boriesky smiled to himself as she grabbed William's ear and toted him away. All this to the chagrin of poor William, who despite his plea of what'd I do, mama? was encountering this very real public embarassment. Some of the villagers, including Mayor Sven, found the spectacle amusing and composure difficult.

Nellie Gilbert's turn came next. She politely put her two jars of perserves into Boriesky's hands and bowed slightly. Hans remained in his seat and Nellie thought it was an act of shyness, of Hans being fearful of approaching the Maestro. Nellie explained it was a gift from her and her son. "Ah, now THIS is a practical gift, madam," Boriesky commented, "when I was a lad I often helped my mother preparing such preserves." He opened one jar, sampling the sweet apricot flavor. "Hmmm...exactly as I remember the way mother made preserves. I commend you, madam, and advise you that fine delicacy could rival my dear mother's own, God rest her soul. Now where is your boy? He should know my appreciation also."

Nellie Gilbert felt a twinge of embarrassment at not knowing why Hans was not at her side. "I am sorry, sir," she offered, "but it seems..."

"I'm right here, mama" she heard Hans say, and noticed he stood at her side holding the box her gathered from the carriage. "Maestro, this is from my father," and he presented Oleg Boriesky with the long, wooden box.

"Another gift from your family? Well, where is your father that I might thank him?"

Nellie Gilbert was taken aback by Hans offering but now realized what was in the box. "Maestro, my deepest apologies, but Hans' father passed away some years back."

Oleg Boriesky was just as confused as anyone nearby who was paying attention to what was occurring. He turned to Hans and saw a look in his eyes that predicated his next move. "Well, lad, if you believe that this is what your father would like me to have, then by all means I accept your generos…" His words drifted away, lost as he opened the lid of the wooden box. There before him, sitting in a bed of fine straw, was Hans' beautiful, golden-brown violin! There was a pause in time for all present as the Maestro sat motionless before this magificent looking instrument. The memory of his father and the wonderful violin that he made for Oleg when he was a lad came streaming forth. This violin from Hans had the same texture, the same balance. He ran his fingers along its golden hue, raised it to his chin, gently tweaked the delicate strings, tuning the keys to bring each one to its correct pitch. "Young lad, what is your name?" Oleg Boriesky inquired.

"Hans. Hans Gilber, sir."

"Master Gilbert. This violin…I have not seen such craftsmanship in many years. What is it's origin? Did your father play?"

"My father played only briefly as a young man. He began work on this violin before he died, and left it to me to complete. I finished it from sketchings he left, and was able to complete it once I learned how to play and discovered what it needed."

Oleg Boriesky pondered what Hans said, holding the violin before him. "If you play, then, young master, then this belongs to you. Never would I part a boy from such a fine possession."

Hans pleaded: "Please, Maestro, accept this gift. I can't explain why I know this but my father would have wanted you to have it. My mother and I are simple farmers and I believe that is what I will always do. Eventually this violin will do nothing but gather dust in a closet and that is not what I finished it for. I wanted it to be heard so that my father's spirit would rejoice everytime it was played."

Oleg moved his gaze from his wife Zocia, then to Hans who now stood before his mother, her arms holding him near. "How could you have known how to construct the intonation?" he asked, "Who taught you the balance, the bridging? It takes craftsman I know a lifetime to learn and some are still not successful."

"I do not know, sir. My father taught me what I know and his spirit guided my hands each moment I worked on it. Maybe God wouldn't let it come out wrong? He made it from his heart as I finished it from mine."

"From your heart? I learned on such a violin, made by my own father's hands, Master Hans. Maybe, just maybe…" and he raised the instrument to his chin, bow in hand, but paused for a moment, then lowered it back down.

"No, Master Hans, this is not right. If I am to hear the essence of this beautiful instrument, then as my father sat before me when I played, so I am asking of you to play for me. Let me hear the true soul of the person that this work of art might have inherited. I beg of you to play for me, for that would truly be the gift I crave."

There comes a time in each of our lives, whether we grow old and bitter, or age with the wisdom of our years that we stand convinced there is more than what we see and hear. If we mutiny against all that we are taught, or have learned, then there will be one moment in time when we will realized that all of everything that is or has been in this universe will be offered to us in one brief, glorious moment. It opens our hearts as we become inundated with the elation and pangs of emotion. It brings back our childhood, our first love, our first broken heart. It vividly recalls for us the first time we held our children, or the sad moment we let them go.

For that one moment we remember a parent's love, a brother or sister's love, friends in our lives, sweethearts, all that life can and has offered is given to each of us again at that one moment in time. The deep snows of winter's past, the bright harvest moons, the rapturous days of youth spent under a sweltering summer's sun - all of that can exist in one torrent of a moment if we are fortunate enought to experience it. Oleg Boresky's moment had come. As Hans' fingers flowed across the strings of the violin, Oleg felt the tears on his face and the grasp of undulated emotion piercing his heart. As Hans played, all else came to not be. The vaulted images of his youth came rushing back. He saw his papa again, smiling and still shedding tears as he did when Oleg played for him, only now... now he understood why. He finally came to know the reason his papa cried so; he cried because the angels cried, these same angels who now cried for Hans' music as he played the music of Heaven. It reached beyond the tent walls, carrying into the distant hills, carrying into the very night sky above.

When Hans stopped playing, there was silence. No, there was awe that amounted to silence and respect. All that were there, the citizens of Capaldi, members of the Molshoi made no sound, no movement in reverence to what they just heard. Oleg Boriesky knew what had to be done, what he had to say: "I cannot accept this violin as a gift, Master Hans."

"But...why sir?" gasped Hans Gilbert.

"Because it's purpose has been fulfilled. You have already given me the greatest gift I could ever have hoped to receive. Your beautiful music has reminded me of the love I once had for my art. It has returned to my soul the very substance of what music was intended for. I suspect this is what your father would have wanted me to have. Whether or not you stay a simple farmer, or move onto greater things, this instrument belongs to its true *Maestro*. That is you, Hans Gilbert." With that, he returned the violin to its wooden box. "But what I will do for you is to ensure you have a proper case for this wondrous instrument. I will see to it that such a case is delivered to you, and then when you come and see me again, you must bring your violin in its own special case and play for me. Do I have your word?"

"Yes, Maestro," Hans promised, "I will always take the greatest care of it."

Afterwards, the evening commenced. Hans Gilbert and his mama rode back to their small farm with little having to be said between them. Nellie Gilbert knew her son was more of a man than she had ever realized. Her heart beamed with pride.

Oleg Boriesky came to appreciate the beauty of the small village of Capaldi, much like the same village he was raised in. How many other small hamlets had he failed to notice these last few years? Soon he would perform before the Duke and the Royal Family. It would be his last performance. Zocia deserved it, he knew she had enough and wanted to go home. Home to where his father shed his tears, and now he could retire contented that he knew why.

Tracks in the Snow

My father and sunrise were synonymous. If I was asked, I wouldn't be able to recall a morning of my youth that by the time I woke my father hadn't already completed one or two chores and walked to the local deli and back for his coffee and paper. By the time I made my dreary-eyed journey downstairs I would always find him sitting on his favorite spot on the couch with a disassembled daily newspaper scattered betwixt the floor and the sofa. This was his style of reading the day's events: through a frontal assault, page-folded-over-page folded as if the paper's dismemberment somehow remedied the all-too bitter news of any given day.

When I was very young, rising early was an easy task, a routine conditioned by mother that I accepted as the normal course of exisitng, no different from breathing. Early mornings bred the unknown adventures of a new day, and I anxiously stood at the helm, willing and able. I was the youngest of six with four sisters and a brother, all of them half-siblings, three of them who were living with us moved out while I was still a lad leaving me to befriend my imagination more than anything, or anyone else. My brother left to join the army and the two sisters that were living in our house were forced out to live with their natural mother. I have memories of them standing in our living room, head-in-hands, crying while my mother yelled in anger at whatever offense they might have committed. I don't even recall a goodbye, they were just gone and it was me and mother alone during the day until father retired from his 40 years of 9-5 monotony. My playmate, more often than not, was the boy I saw in the bathroom mirror.

Morning snowfall was a particular favorite of mine during the cold, winter months. I would anticipate the crunch of the newly fallen pile beneath my boots; often looking back to see the fresh path I had created. In my youthful ambition of adventure I would discover the tracks of many of God's creatures such as cats, birds, rabbits or possum. I felt pity for the cats, imagining they were estranged from their warm homes and were being sought desperately by their heart-broken owners. These very same cats now had to fend for themselves through the dreadnought of winter's weather that was not merciful to any animals raised and bred in the creature comforts that their owners provided for them. There were other animal prints I didn't recognize, and I reasoned they belonged to creatures of the nearby meadows that dared venture near our homes in search of food. I suspected many a misplaced feline became the meal of a voracious carnivore, just before leaving the evidence of its footprints in our front yard.

Of course, there were always father's tracks, his footprints finding their way down our front steps, disappearing down the hill, then back again and up the steps to our front door. From outside on our porch, as I shivered off the initial shock of the cold morning air, I could see dad through the living room window with his coffee and paper at his usual spot on the couch. Some think this is a harsh memory of my father, others see it as trivial, but it is still my memory. It belongs to me as much as the domain of those outside snowy days were mine and mine alone. I have no private moments with dad to share, no stories that I can tell my children. He just wasn't that type of father. Years later I would realize he was there because it was easier, more comfortable than not being there. Living in our house, paying the bills, fixing what needed fixing worked for him as long as his meals were cooked, his clothes washed, and mom picked up the scattered remnants of the daily paper from the living room floor. There was no need to play catch with his son, build a snowman, or any of the standard father-son activities I'd read about in all the Dick and Jane books, or my Highlights magazine. The TV shows of my youth enhanced this illusion - Leave it to Beaver, Father Knows Best, the Andy Griffith Show - they were catalysts of a fantasy world, but weren't part of my reality. His contentment, or resignation of what his life had become didn't even allow him to fight for his own daughters, rather to keep quiet and accept they no longer lived in his house than to arouse the ire of mother.

Mother's mornings were very different. She generally ached, moaned and groaned with the symptoms of some oncoming imagined illness, or else she expounded the demerits of surviving with little or no sleep. Mother claimed for years that each night offered her an hour or two of rest at the most, and she just didn't know how she would get through the day, but she always did and usually with more energy then I ever displayed.

Mom also grew anxious if anyone in the house slept when she was awake, and she had this habit, subtle or not, of assuring that all left dreamland behind when she walked the floors with a heavy step. I remember many a morning being slowly roused from sleep to find her in my room and well into a conversation with me, obviously begun while I still lay entrenched in slumber. This became a problem when as a young man I made my living as a musician playing in after-hours clubs six-nights a week, often crawling into bed around 5 a.m. It was a tiring but profitable livelihood to all but mother. She thought it out of place sleeping past 7a.m., awakening me with the disciplined warning of procuring a 9-to-5 vocation, a "real job", or else. Frequently, it meant condescending, getting dressed and leaving to find sleep at an understanding friend's house.

Finally, out of the necessity of health and sanity I explained the problem to dad who thought I had a lifetime of work ahead but like all of us, just a few short years to pursue my dreams and there was no need to dive into the daily grind just yet. He demanded of mother to let me be in the mornings, and she reluctantly agreed, though she became convinced my sleeping through the noon hour was not due to hard work, but rather to the onset of a "perilous lifestyle to which my nights were becoming accustomed!". It was a battle fought and won by my father and why he reserved his defense for me and not my sisters was never answered. In time my late-night hours gave way to more conventional means of support for myself and eventually to my own family that relied on me, but mom never deviated from her sunrise wanderings. Without me there, poor father had become the target of her early morning domicile anxieties. He once told me that his morning walks started a bit earlier and took a bit longer than they did before.

So I guess it was almost fitting that when I got the call from my sister the day was still so young. She said dad had been stricken, collapsing at the deli as he paid for his coffee, and I should come right away. She said mom would not go to the hospital with anyone but me.

It took time for me to get there with the as yet unplowed roads, but when I pulled in front of the house there was mom looking jittery and scared, waiting for me on the front porch. I ran to help her to my truck.

"He slept late," she said, "he was just too tired to get up, but I told him there was cleaning I had to do and he'd be in the way…it's all my fault!"

"Now, mom, it's no one's fault," I tried to assure her, but I easily envisioned how dad journeyed to the store against his better judgment just to escape her nagging.

As we moved carefully down the snowy steps, I noticed several animal tracks, being filled-in now by the falling snow, and father's boot prints disappearing, as was their custom, down the hill.

The Messiah of Harriman

Prologue

Sergeant Thomas O'Malley was tired. It was 5:30am and no matter how many times in so many years he'd been on the job he could not adjust to getting up so early. He drank his coffee, and, as usual it tasted like mud, or at least what he imagined mud tasted like. Thomas O'Malley dumped most of it into the sink and planned on picking up a cup at the deli as he did every morning. Damn, never could make a cup of coffee, he thought. Not like Mary...now Mary could make coffee!

For eighteen years, virtually every morning she came to his thoughts. Eighteen long years of tears and hurt he's endured since she left him after Thomas Jr disappeared. She blamed him for it, for everything, and who could blame her for believing that, he thought. The boy wanted to hunt, wanted to hunt with his dad more than anything else. He would sit wide-eyed and proud, listening to his father's stories when he spoke about the woods and the animals. Each time, though, there was an excuse not to bring Thomas Jr. along: it was always next year, you're too young...it's just the men going, and each time Thomas Jr. was left behind with his shattered dreams and hopes...except the last time.

It was April, eighteen years ago in the middle of a stormy night that Thomas Jr. slipped away. A confused boy of twelve, full of anguish and frustration, he'd show his father he could hunt! He took his backpack with the Superman logo on it, and the old Remington his dad gave him. He planned on bringing back a good-sized buck. Maybe even a bear! The rain didn't bother him. Heck, his dad was out there and just like him Thomas Jr. had good rain gear to wear. He slipped it on and left silently through his bedroom window. Sure, mom would be mad. After all, that's what mom's do, but he had to do this to show his father he was a man.

Mary O'Malley woke before dawn, something startled her from sleep. She always slept uneasy when Tom Sr. was away, but this anxiety, for some reason, was stronger. Maybe a noise woke her, or a bad dream: she couldn't tell. But now she was awake so she grabbed her robe to check on the boy. Maybe he called her and her maternal instincts reacted to arouse her from her fitful sleep. She peeked into this bedroom, startled by what she found: an empty bed, his pajamas strewn on the floor and the bedroom window open. Trying not to panic, she ran to the bathroom, praying he might be there, but he wasn't, and he wasn't in the kitchen, the living room, or anywhere else in the house. "Thomas" she yelled, "Tommy, where are you?" She continued yelling, running from room-to-room, then out the back door into the blistering rain. She called again and again, waited, then yelled again but received no answer. Around the house she ran, yelling and pushing herself through the mud that clung to her slippers and robe, slowing her down to a struggle. With no reply she ran back into the house, upstairs into Thomas Jr's bedroom. She knew all about her boy, all he was, and all he had, and with this she scampered through his closet to realize her fears were true: the boy's gun was gone, along with his rain gear, backpack and one-man tent. Down the stairs she ran, grabbing the phone and cranking it hard for an operator to get her the police.

"Police headquarters, Officer Williams". (Thank God, Mary thought), "Glenn! It's Mary O'Malley. It's Thomas Jr, he's run off! Tom Sr is away hunting and I think he went to find him. Help me, Glenn…I don't know where he is…"

"We're on our way, Mrs O'Malley" the officer replied. Back on the front porch, in the pouring rain, she sank to a step with her head in her hands, crying for help, for God's help, for her boy. A few moments later, the police arrived.

They never found Thomas Jr, Every available officer and civilian, using both dogs and planes searched Harriman Park for weeks on end but hope eventually ran out. The rescue mission for Thomas Jr become a recovery mission, but to no avail. The nights in early spring were still cold, and a young boy surviving with almost nothing for an extended period of time was doubtful. Thomas O'Malley Sr became a man obsessed in the search for his son, not going home for days on end except for what he needed to continue. The futility and hopelessness set in over time. He cursed and denied his God for what was taken from him. What he couldn't understand was why he was allowed to survive a war with German ammo exploding all around him and not a scratch only to endure the greatest pain a father could ever experience?

That was eighteen years ago.

Mary never said a word, just left and moved back to her parent's. Even at Thomas Jr's memorial service she took no notice of Thomas Sr, refused to even talk to him, and that tore away a part he never regained. Mary passed away a few years later, cancer the doctors said. By the time he found this out she lay dying in a hospital bed. He raced to be with her one last time but she was already gone. Thomas Sr hoped someone would tell him Mary called his name in those last, ebbing moments, but no one said anything. He still doesn't know why he didn't ask.

Sergeant O'Malley poured his coffee down the kitchen sink, grabbed his jacket and left for work. Once again, he had to put his memories behind him and concentrate on the day's work ahead. First thing came to his mind was the boy at Tiorati who almost drowned yesterday but was pulled through. Pretty routine, except Caso's report had people at the scene talking about the guy who saved him: long hair, a beard, raggedy clothes. Probably a vagrant living in the park somewhere. Well, he'd have to find him if that's the case and have him shipped out, can't have strays making themselves comfortable in a state park, the chief would have his head. But he couldn't be too bad if he saved the boy's life. The sargeant would have his officers keep an eye open and bring him in if they find him.

I

> In the clearing misty morn, ,
> from petal to petal, raindrop
> to raindrop against dew-
> laden leaves, brisk-running
> streams, and a newly-awakened sun…

I See Him

It was so beautiful here at dawn. The water like flawless glass began at his feet and disappeared in the early morning mist somewhere near the opposite shore. He kneeled at the water's edge moving slowly in the glowing luster of the rising sun. Before him, the wisps on the water's cool surface began to change, to take form. Slowly they took the shape of cherubs, crying for him. They knew it was time. Their soft, beautiful faces streamed with tears that fell to the earth as dewdrops. He sensed they mourned the path that lay before him, but when their arms reached out, he quickly rose to his feet. The day was beginning, his journey was settling to its close. As he walked towards the nearby road he marveled at all that there was around him, marveled at the sun's glory and the pureness of the morning air, at the sweet birdsongs that heralded in his honor. Yet, he was saddened. This stranger knew it was time to begin the longest way home one could ever know.

II

Damn, it was cold this morning! Jim dug down deep into his bag for the flannel shirt he was now glad he remembered to bring. He laid his fishing pole down on the boat's bottom and donned the shirt. Eddie was of a heartier breed and the chilly morning air each time they went fishing never seemed to bother him. Eddie was changing lures because the topwater he was using wasn't working as well as he had hoped. "Better off using a spoon with a pork trailer" he said aloud to no one but himself, really, but Jimmy got the idea.

"Ain't you cold, buddy?" Jim asked, but Eddie didn't answer. He never answered the same question Jim asked each time they were out. His only response to Jimmy everytime was "faggot-ass", mocking him for not having the tolerance that he had to the frigid early Spring morning.

Eddie liked their location. There was a felled tree nearby that was partially in the lake. It looked like an excellent cover for Bass. He cast his silver spoon slightly upstream from the tree and planned to work it gingerly down past the structure, hoping to entice any fish that was looking for easy prey. The cast was perfect, maybe five to seven feet beyond the timber. Eddie waited for the spoon to hit bottom and for the ripples on the water to dissipate before he began his "jigging" motion, pulling the lure slowly towards the boat, causing it to bounce up and down beneath the surface.

It was then he noticed the lone figure strolling along the nearby road. They weren't anywhere near the campsites here in Harriman, so this fellow was out doing some serious walking. Jim became aware of the figure on the shore when the stranger stopped and took notice of them. He walked to the water's edge and raised his hand in greeting. "How ya doin'" Jim said to the man on the shore. "Beautiful mornin', huh?" he added.

"Every morning is beautiful in my Father's kingdom" the stranger replied back. Oh great, a religious nut, thought Eddie, out here in the middle of nowhere. "Yeah, I guess it would be" Eddie responded.

"God bless you my good man" the stranger added, and turned again towards the road.

"Geez" Jim remarked, "guess he's a happy camper. Not feeling any pain, if you know what I mean".

"That's the truth…" Eddie began to add when the line on his fishing pole whirred with the promise of a good catch. He grabbed the pole and began the motion of trying to bring into the boat what it was that attached itself to his lure. He reeled down and pulled up, over and over again. Jimmy shouted encouragement, offering advice, as fishermen are wont to do towards others that find themselves in such a battle. Eddie had to let a bit of line out to let the fish run with it. It was the only way he could avoid his line being snapped, by letting the fish tire himself out before Eddie began reeling him in again. "Damn, Eddie. You got a monster!" Jim said anxiously.

"That's what she said" Eddie replied. It was the stock sportsmen reply to any comment that referenced size. They both enjoyed a laugh at Eddie's crude comment when they were able to get a glimpse of the fish Eddie now had near the boat. It was a Bass, all right; biggest damn Bass either of them had ever seen outside of a sport show's stuffed and mounted exhibits.

"My God", Jim said, "Ed, I think you might have a record here" as Eddie was now holding the big fish with two hands, one grabbing the bottom lip, the other the belly.

"It's a female", Eddie told Jim, "look at her belly. Ready to spawn it looks like". As he said this, Eddie noticed the stranger still strolling slowly down the road, looking back at him. Even as far away as He was, Eddie couldn't help but take notice of his eyes. They seemed black, yet he could have sworn they were blue when the stranger stood near to their boat on the shore. He noticed the eyes on the Bass were also a deep black, a black that resonated somewhere in Eddie's soul.

"We gotta put her back" he told Jim.

"You crazy! How many times in your life you gonna land something like this. We should take her to the bait shop in town and have her weighed, man", Jim responded, but Eddie took no heed. He lowered the large fish back into the water and watched as she slowly swam away, staying on the surface for a while before diving down into the dark water. He looked up again at the stranger who had stopped walking once more to see Eddie return the Bass to the lake. The stranger smiled at Eddie who no longer saw the deep black eyes he saw before. He couldn't make them out at all from this distance.

"I'll be damned" he said softly, to no one but himself.

III

Brrr! The water felt colder than it did before lunch Bobby thought, but he'd get used to it. After all, little boys adjust quickly to cool water when it means playtime. He loved this place, Lake Ti-ratty, or something like that dad called it, but what's in a name to a ten-year old? Funny how mom said to wait awhile before going back in the water after so big a lunch. That's a strange rule, Bobby thought, and what a lunch it was too! Hot dogs, fried chicken, potato salad, soda pop, ice-cream and watermelon. He and mom and dad ate a whole watermelon! .

Anyway, he felt real good and wanted to swim out to the ropes where those floating things were attached. "I can do it," thought Bobby. He did it once with dad and now it was an adventure and adventures are what ten-year old boys must have, so he began to swim.

Bobby kicked his feet and splashed his arms down until his body became parallel with the muddy bottom. He kicked and splashed vigorously towards the ropes, but Bobby didn't remember them being so far. In a short while they proved to be too far and his body needed rest, but he couldn't stand on the lake's bottom now, it was too far down and he sank, losing his breath, gasping and fighting to climb upwards toward an unclear light. Bobby was kicking and screaming and trying to yell when so much water rushed down his throat, and so much blackness overcame his little boy mind that the light overhead disappeared. The pain and the blackness didn't matter anymore.

It was the children on the beach who first saw Bobby Barringer fighting for his life. They screamed and pointed, some cried while Bobby struggled when the adults on shore became aware of what was happening. Bobby's father, Peter, raced into the water with the other men while his frenzied wife yelled deliriously from the shore.

They carried Bobby's motionless body out of the water and laid him gently down as a crowd gathered. His mother clutched his still body. Someone who knew CPR began working on Bobby desperately, putting him first on his stomach, then to his side lifting the boy's arms and pushing on his upper back to get the water out. He turned Bobby over, pinching his nostrils while gently blowing precious air into his lungs. Over and over again before a restless crowd the procedure continued but Bobby didn't respond. His screaming mother was restrained by a friend while an unbelieving father took over the CPR, lifting, pushing, blowing... but Bobby did not move, he didn't cry out or cough. He didn't do anything but remain limp and motionless. The children cried while the gathered adults looked on with resolution that the boy would not wake up. He was gone and they all knew it. Someone raced back to the crowd to tell them that they called for help but they all knew it was too late. A grieving mother and father both kneeled down over their son and held him, sobbing loudly to God that this can't be and that it wasn't fair.

It was then it happened. Those who were there can attest to it. Someone from out of nowhere came and lifted Bobby's parents off of him. Peter Barringer fought, but this stranger's grasp was so strong and so assuring in some way, it felt the right thing to do. Peter moved away and held onto his wife while the stranger bent over the boy. No one moved to stop him, no one thought they should. Where did he come from, they thought? This tattered stranger in bare feet was now kneeling down over Bobby Barringer, holding the boy's head and stroking his hair softly, gently, while whispering something to him that was too low for anyone to hear.

The boy coughed. Then he coughed again, and again. His mother grabbed hold of him in her arms, tears of joy running down her face while her little boy continued to cough and slowly become conscious of where he was. A stunned Peter Barringer held them both while the gathered crowd stood stunned in silent surprise by what they just saw.

An emergency squad arrived at the scene. The crowd parted a path for their arrival. Two police officers also appeared, one of them Officer Matt Caso got the details and called them into headquarters. His partner sat in the patrol car listening to his report of a boy who drowned and by all accounts was dead when some guy jumps in and brings the kid through doing nothing more than stroking his head, but now the guy is nowhere to be found. No one ever saw him before and no one saw him leave, but he was gone. Some old lady insisted it was an angel and the boys' parents didn't disagree with her. They would have believed anything that brought their boy back.

No, the kid was fine Officer Caso reported, didn't need any further medical attention and the parent's just wanted to take him home. The weird part was the boy kept saying something about the "light that saved him". Officer Caso concluded his report, and he and his partner joked about what the Sarge would say when they got back to the station. Still, it was a callout to remember and it did have a good ending. Thank God for that.

IV

> Now and forever, from every note I can
> sing, to every song I hear, from
> the rapture of the wind to the sweet
> melody of a child's tender whisper...

I Hear Him

When the sun rose higher overhead, he sat by the lake away from the beach. Here the stranger could watch the children playing, their parents performing the duties a picnic required were gathered at the tables on the nearby clearing.

The stranger loved to watch children. They were of a pureness he understood, so refreshing, so cleansed. He noticed then a young boy out in the water so far from the rest and beginning to struggle and he felt angry. He knew the demons that pursued him would do anything to draw him out, even use this child. He watched as the men on the beach raced into the water and brought the boy's unmoving body to shore. The stranger raced along the shoreline, watching the futile attempts at reviving the boy. His anger became pitched.

He moved the father aside and knelt to touch the child's head, feeling for him in that black void he knew the child had gone to, that place where he was forced to retreat to. It was there the stranger found Bobby Barringer.

He offered the boy a light, a bright light to remove the blackness and he called for him to come towards it, assuring Bobby it was all right now. Finally, the boy arrived and he woke, choking from the water that sat in his ten-year old lungs. The stranger moved aside for the boy's parents and slipped quickly back through the crowd to seek rest.

The demons had drained him already and he needed rest. His day was only beginning.

V

Phillip Richmond was seventy-four years old. He lived with Phillip Jr and his family. Phillip Sr was a stout, elderly but robust man and other than the Europe he saw during the Great War, his life has always been here in Sloatsburg.

He's been a widower for twelve years now; the good Lord took his Jenny from him, but He was merciful. She suffered for so long, and he watched her day-in and day-out endure all that pain. He helped her pray for it all to end, and it did end...for Jenny. For Phillip Sr, as it is for all of us left behind, the pain never ends. It gets tucked away in a corner of the heart, or behind a door in the brain, but it never truly leaves.

Phillip Sr was also blind, for six years now. "Dang fool blind" he called it. You see, there was this fall off the old back porch. Late, when it was dark. His old cat Amos was to blame. Seems she hadn't come home that night as she usually did and Phillip remembers hearing her call, like an ailing call, in the dark. A call for help. So, in his haste he tried to rush to help Amos and tripped over something, smashing through the porch's rail to the garden below. Robert, his oldest grandson heard the crash and came running, finding his grandfather unconscious. He called Phillip Jr for help.

Afterwards, Phillip Sr remembers waking up, or at least it seemed like waking up, lying on a bed somewhere, and it was very dark. Soon, he realized his eyes were covered, that his head had been bandaged and he began to stir, sitting up with a start. "It's alright, pop", and he felt Phil Jr's hands gently grabbing his own and lowering his head back onto the pillow.

"What is this, Philly? What happened to me?" Phil Sr anxiously inquired.

"Pop, you had a fall, hit your head on a rock and Robbie found you. You're in the hospital now and it's going to be okay." Good ol' Philly, he thought, he was real proud of his son. He grew to be such a strong man, knows how to earn his keep in this world. Jenny was dang proud of him too! She gave him the name Philly, says it was after his favorite baseball team. "Listen, pop...Dr Geoffries is here now, and he wants to talk to you. I'll be nearby if you need me." Phil Jr released his father's hand and stepped out into the hallway.

"James?" Phil Sr asked aloud, "that you?"

"I'm here, Phil." James Geoffries and Phil Richmond went back a long ways. From the same small town, same age, they both courted Jenny when Teddy Roosevelt was in charge. Phil Sr always wondered why she chose him, a steel worker, when she could have married a doctor. He and James stayed close till Jenny died, then Phil Sr forgot about the rest of the world.

"Why these fool bandages over my eyes, James? I feel fine...maybe a mule-kick of a headache, but dang! Felt worse after having a few too many."

James Geoffries had been the Richmond family doctor every year since he'd been in practice. He delivered Phil Jr and Robert, set Phil Sr's busted leg after his tractor accident, attended to Jenny faithfully while she struggled through the illness that eventually took her life. Telling his old friend now that he was probably going to be blind for the rest of his life was painful. "I'm sorry, Phil" he told his old friend, "I wish there was more I could do."

Phil Sr at first said nothing. The room was a loud silent as he pondered the information he'd just received. "Well, James, I guess it is what it is. I've only my fool self to blame."

"Grampa, grampa! I saw that big, brown rabbit today!" Phil Sr's granddaughter Jenny excitedly exclaimed. Named after her grandmother, she was the love of Phil Sr's life.

"Did you now?" responded Phil Sr, "Well, I'll bet he'll make fine stew one day."

"Oh, grampa, don't say that! I couldn't never, ever eat him." Of all the most agonizing things about being blind to Phil Sr, worse that not seeing the sunrise or the first frost of winter, was not being able to see his precious granddaughter's face. She loved her grandfather, sitting with him and listening to all of his stories of her daddy when he was a little boy, of grandma whom she'd seen pictures of: she loved all the wonderful things grampa would tell her.

Phil would ever-so-lightly run his fingers over her tiny features, sculpting her image indelibly into his mind. She must be so beautiful, he thought, but he felt pain in his heart from his desire to see her. He wanted to see the green in her eyes, the brown of her long, curly hair, the pink of those tiny cheeks. His hands could never "feel" those parts of this child. "Come, grampa, he might still be out back. Maybe we could find him!" Jenny said anxiously.

"Take my hand, Jenny. Don't go moving too fast now. Where are we headin'?"

"Out by the old shed, grampa. He went under it." Jenny took Phil Sr by the hand and led him out back. The old shed was the Richmond's smoke house, not being used, really, for anything any longer. It was at the end of the property, at the edge of a tree line which served as the boundary for Harriman State Park. The Village of Sloatsburg asked him once a long time ago to please take the shed down, but he refused, said it was there long before the park and will return to the earth when she takes it back. Now he was heading there with his granddaughter. "You sit here, grampa. I'll go look," Jenny exclaimed excitedly.

"Not too far, child. Stay within my hearing," he called back as he sat down on the old shed bench. How rickety it was! But it must have been here near fifty years Phil Sr thought. Then Jenny called to him.

"There he goes, grampa. Over the hill! I'll catch him." The 'hill' Jenny was shouting about was a steep, grassy knoll on the south side of the shed. It ran down to a fast moving, wide stream. Too dangerous a place for Jenny.

"No, Jenny. Let him be! Come back here. Jenny!" Phil yelled. He found his way to the shed's corner and began edging towards the direction of her voice. A few feet later he stumbled, fell to the soft earth, then started crawling. He yelled again with as loud a voice as he could: "Jenny. Jenny baby. Come back to grampa, Jen…"

It was that moment Phil Sr felt hands on his shoulders, lifting him to his feet. "Phil, is that you? Robert? Get Jenny. She's chasing that dang rabbit by the stream. She's…"

"Do not fear," Phil Sr heard in an unfamiliar voice, "the child is safe. You've only to see for yourself."

Phillip Richmond Sr's senses reeled. Such a voice he had never heard before. Who was this man? He lifted his hands to feel for a familiar feature, but a strong, assuring grip lowered them down. His head was spinning. The all-encompassing black he lived with began turning to gray. He was able to distinguish countless points of flashing yellow lights that became white and grew larger. They were followed by a blinding white and Phil Sr screamed from the glare. The form of a man began shaping itself within the white light. A form that grew distinct, defined, then began fading.

"The child calls you," the stranger said sternly, and he gently turned Phil Sr's head, back towards the direction of Jenny's voice. The glaring white before him began to dissipate and in its dying more shapes formed: distant and nearby structures that he recognized. The grassy knoll was before him, he could see it! He could see the blue sky, the green grass, the trees without number, and the clouds above him seemed within his reach.

"Grampa, are you okay? Who was that man?" Jenny inquired, frightened by her grandfather's excited state though she couldn't tell just yet what was changed about him. Phil Sr fell to his knees. He held her in his arms, hugging her tightly, then holding her at arm's length, soaking in her loveliness, prettier than he ever imagined she would be.

"It's alright, Jenny. It's alright. Run and get daddy," Phil Sr urged the child, "and hurry now." Something exciting was happening, and Jenny was no longer frightened. She could tell it was a happy something and she ran yelling for her father. Phil Sr reveled in her tiny form running towards the house and disappearing through the back door. Then he remembered the man, the one who had helped him up. He scanned the property from where he stood and could find no one. "Hello," he called, then called again to absolute silence. He looked back at the old shed and there sitting by the corner near the property's fence was that big, brown rabbit Jenny had been chasing. The creature bounded off through a hole in the fence and into the park. Phil Sr turned to see his family running towards him. Dang if that rabbit didn't smile at him before it took off, he thought.

VI

Life is the path. Love is the
only key to understanding every
living thing, every form of
His happiness. Through this…

I Know Him

He had known about this old one. In church, this man sang loudly to the Heavens, his voice uplifting in spirit the faith in God above. This man, who had seemingly lost so much, lost not an ounce of love for the Father, and now he carried this love for his granddaughter. This old one wanted her image before him more than life itself, but never begrudged the fates that refused him.

The stranger could feel the pangs of mercy in his heart for this old man, and that day as he stood among the trees and watched him frolic about with this beautiful child he chose to grant him his greatest desire. The stranger knew there was much at stake, but more than his task was his caring for the people. They were his reason, and his cause, and if such a blessing could be done for one of such faith he felt assured the Almighty would understand and approve. He gave this elder his sight, restored the visage of his granddaughter to him. Afterwards, drained and depleted, he staggered to a nearby stream, falling into its cool waters. His heart beat rapidly, his body ached and his head throbbed with pain and confusion.

"My Father, have I wronged you? he cried out,"Then leave me not with these choices! Let my will be your bidding. Let…" and he collapsed from the pain that coursed through his head. Soon, he heard voices. Men were coming. Not like this, he thought, I am not ready, and he frantically scrambled to his feet and stole away, deeper into the forest where he felt safe. In a small clearing he laid back down. Frightened and lonely for the first time, he fell asleep and dreamed of kingdoms of gold, and jeweled crowns, and beautiful women.

VII

Margaret Anna Magdalan sat staring at the blank sheet of paper in the typewriter before her for what must have been hours. It was writer's block, and it happened too often to her lately. Her "At Home with Maggie" column for the local paper, the Sloatsburg Daily, would once again be late. Once again she'd hear hell and once again Maggie would give assurances to her editor it would not happen again.

After all these years of giving those stay-at-home wives ways to make the daily drudgery easier with her household tips, the well was running dry. Hell, she thought, she didn't aspire to be a journalist for this crap anyway, but the years slipped past so quickly. "Just start with this column," her editor said years ago, "then we can move on to bigger assignments." And she waited and waited, got comfortable with a steady paycheck, her column became popular, and always thought there'd be time to move up or move on.

Maggie trudged her fifty-six year old body from the kitchen to the bedroom. Might as well jump into the shower, she thought. She undressed, standing naked in front of the full-length mirror that hung on her bedroom door. Maggie never thought herself as being beautiful at any point in time, but once she held pride for having a shapely, firm, young body. The kind that made it easy to read the minds of men who were nearby. God, how she let herself go, and why not? There was no husband to look good for, no children or grandchildren she had to keep pace with. There was only herself and she lost interest long ago.

She was alone in this big world, except for a cousin that lived in Pennsylvania, and she didn't know anything about her, being years since they even spoke. Maggie's life was her job, but now, though, that job was taking its toll. She was aging into a lonesome spinster. Oh, letters from readers with their problems seeking her help came in often enough, and to which she occasionally provided a brilliant solution: these kept her weekly column popular. To them, thought Maggie, she was only a by-line on a column they read after the news, sports pages, comics and Dear Abbie. But it wasn't always like this.

Maggie remembers years ago there was Joseph. It was such a typical love-lost story. They were both young and very much together. Joe was tall, strong and handsome. He was also ambitious, but it was a driving ambition that never sought direction. He was able to do a bit of everything but failed to master anything. He feared falling into the trap of living a life in a small town and Maggie remembers their last conversation. "But you have to come with me," he pleaded, standing on the train platform. But, she didn't go with him, she had dreams of her own and they seemed so close, so within reach. When your dreams are so near, each move causes anxiety, or fear that any move might be the wrong move. Maggie was just getting started with the newspaper, her editor assured her she would do fine but she had to keep working. She couldn't leave, not now. She had worked too hard.

That rainy October afternoon at the train station she stood under her umbrella on the platform. The train that carried Joe had already left; she watched it grow smaller in the distance. Already, Maggie felt lonely, like she was in an old movie, except Joseph did not wave goodbye from the last car, he didn't want to watch her fade away. Instead, he stayed inside the train car, heading for a wide world of whatever, leaving behind his memory and his heart.

VIII

Maggie dried herself off after the shower and got dressed. She heard the rain against her windows as she once again was before her typewriter, adjusting her seat, moving the items on her desk. All the time thinking that something would come to her, some new inspiration would gel. Several hours passed. She stared at the blank sheet that sat in the typewriter's carriage before her. It was no use so she resigned herself to a lost cause and began putting everything away believing next time would be better. Moving the papers on her desk she came across a small newspaper clipping she had saved. It was about a boy who nearly drowned at Tiorati a few weeks back. The boy was pulled to shore but given up as lost, despite all the efforts of everyone there until a man took the boy in his arms and resuscitated him, not through mouth-to-mouth or any other emergency procedure, but simply by stroking the boy's hair and speaking softly to him. The article said the boy's rescuer disappeared during the excitement of the boy's recovery and no one present noticed him gone. The parents thanked this stranger in the newspaper, if he should read it. Further underneath the clipping were some notes she scribbled herself about Phil Richmond. They were quotes from Dr Geoffrey about Phil being able to see again. Maggie paid the doctor a visit after hearing the rumor; she had known the Richmond family since she was a young girl living in the same neighborhood in Sloatburg. In a small town there weren't many rumors that escaped her and Dr Geoffrey said that yes, it was true, Phil Sr regained his sight. It happened after another fall the doctor said, but the strangest part was what Phil Sr said what happened. He kept insisting there was a man there who helped him up after he fell, a man who Phil Sr swears was somehow responsible for his sight returning. Phil Sr could not describe the stranger, said his vision was still blurry as the man left, but he adamantly maintains the man was real. The doctor told Maggie the most puzzling part was how clean the optical nerves now were, no signs of previous damage. "I've read of similar cases," Dr Geoffrey was quoted, "the nerves slowly heal and it takes a shock or traumatic jolt to actually restore the sight. I've just never come across one like Phil Richmond's case."

Maggie looked at her notes, then back to the newspaper clipping. Was it the same man? Something compelled her curiosity, along with the stories that followed Phil Richmond's and the reports of this stranger in Harriman Park. If he was real, maybe he held a story of sorts, something unique that her editor would approve of, and maybe if she produced it she could prove there was more to her make-up than household hints. She glanced out of her window, noticed it was still raining. Common sense was telling her to wait, that tomorrow in the light of the day it would be a better time, but she did nothing once before, standing on a train platform under wet skies and it cost her dearly. She couldn't take that chance again. She grabbed her bag, put on her raincoat and headed out into the wet, cool evening. Insane, she thought, what do I expect to find? A crackling of thunder boomed overhead as she pulled her car out of the driveway and drove into the night.

It was always the driver's side windshield wiper that was the first to go, everyone knew that. Thank God it wasn't raining very hard, thought Maggie, and the wiper worked somewhat but you had to bend down low to look just over the steering wheel to find the only clear spot on the windshield. She never remembered Seven Lakes Drive being so dark, or so long, seemingly moreso with this aimless journey she was on with no particular destination. Deer occasionally appeared on the roadside but they darted away when her car approached. Maggie came to the first circle, the cut-off for Lake Welch, and hesitated, looking for what? Desperately, in the dark, she needed a decision as to which way to go. Maggie chose straight ahead, going onto Seven Lakes Parkway. The road cuts through the forested state park, showing a lake here and there, and concluding at Lake Tiorati's north end in another traffic circle. Here was a picture of three roads, all scaling upwards, all perilous at night in such weather and here Maggie stopped again. Confused and feeling foolish, it was probably time to turn back, but there was something to be said for coming so far and leaving empty-handed, so she chose the left, or east road for the trek onwards.

Now she'd done it! A sharp left curve here, a sudden right there, and barely able to see. Maggie was scared and couldn't find the room on the dark road to turn the car around. Restlessness turned to fear and fear to panic. Maggie responded by a heavier foot on the accelerator. Getting off this road first seemed the answer, there had to be a place to turn around, but on a right turn she took too fast a large doe stood directly in the center of the narrow road. Blinded by the car's high-beams, it froze. Maggie slammed on her brakes and tried veering to the right to avoid the impact but the right-side provided an incline, a five-foot ditch that brought the car down quickly to a sudden halt, smashing against the upgrade on the far side. A scream was all Maggie could do until her head hit the steering wheel and everything in her world went black.

IX

The heat of the flames from a small campfire stirred Maggie from her sleep. She opened her eyes wide in amazement and confusion as she fought that initial amnesiac onset of where was she and how did she get here? Trying to sit up quickly brought a light-headed feeling, so she eased slowly to a sitting position against a stone wall. She discovered she was lying on an old blanket spread underneath her over a dirt floor. Something with a vinyl feel, stuffed with leaves and grass served as pillow for her head. Whatever it was had seen better days. There was an image imprinted on the ragged material but she couldn't make it out. It contained faded colors, like red and blue. Putting a hand to her head she felt a soft cloth wrapped around it. Her head ached to the touch and she realized the bandage covered a bruise, and now Maggie recalled the accident. She was avoiding a deer in the road…that was all she could remember. Under the bandage were crumpled leaves of some sort over her bruise. Maggie pulled them out, took the cloth off of her head, and struggled to grasp where she was.

Above the flames of the fire she could distinguish somewhat of her surroundings. About twenty-feet opposite her was another stone wall that continued upward twenty to twenty-five feet, then arced towards her, joining the wall she was leaning against, to form a ceiling of natural stone. To Maggie's right, another wall did the same. It was a cave. "But how…?" To her left, a short distance away, was an opening, about ten-feet wide, seven-feet in height. At the entrance to this cave a lone figure of a man sat cross-legged, hands in his lap, not completely showing his whole back, but facing outwards, silhouetted against a blanket of stars in an evening sky. Maggie's heart began beating rapidly, she felt her mouth very dry from the fear as she tried to talk. "Hello," she could barely whisper.

The stranger did not move.

"Hello…?" she said again, louder, hearing the trembling in her voice. Again, no motion from the stranger, no indication he heard her at all. Panic began rearing its ugly head. Maggie looked around the cave for something, anything that she could use to defend herself. "Who are you?" Wh…where am I? Answer me, dammit!" she now demanded.

"I am glad you are alright," the stranger finally offered, "please, if you can, come sit next to me. It is a beautiful evening."

That voice! Sit next to him? All instincts told Maggie to flee, do what she can to get away, but there was something in the way this man spoke, a voice that resonated peace, that offered no reason to fear. Her doubts quickly vanished, the trembling ceased and her heartbeat returned to normal. His was such a trusting, soothing voice, like a child's yet so assuring and commanding in tone. She found herself seated on the ground next to him, waiting for him to turn his head, but he continued his stargazing. She noticed, from the light of the fire, he was a young man, maybe not more than thirty, with a finely-chiseled profile and a shadow of a beard on his face. His hair was dark and long, nearly shoulder-length. Something she had never seen in a man before. The stranger wore an old flannel shirt, much too large for his frame, along with workmen's pants. His feet were bare. Maggie turned her eyes away and outwards. She saw the cave was up high, embedded in a hillside she was unfamiliar with. A slight grade, not too steep, spread down before her. Nothing looked recognizable. How did she get here? Surely, this young man could not have carried her up here by himself?

"Why are you here, Margaret Magdalan?" The question startled her. How could he have known my name? Collecting her thoughts, she noticed her handbag was not in the cave. He must have gone through my purse, found my driver's license. That's it!

"I...I thought you brought me here? From my car, after I ran off the road and knocked myself unconscious. Didn't you find me and carry me to this cave?"

The stranger chose silence again, still staring into space. For what seemed like endless moments later, he spoke: "Isn't it me that you have come looking for?"

What? How? Of course, the newspaper clippings and notes she had in her handbag. He must have found them, along with her license. "Yes. Yes, you are. If you are the man the people of Sloatsburg are talking about, the one who helped that boy at the lake and the person who the blind man swears…"

"I am he," the stranger interrupted.

Finally, Maggie thought, I've found him. But now what? Her journalistic training taught her when the moment is blank, go back to the basics. "Your name? What are you called" she asked.

"People have called me many things," he responded. "but what I was originally named has been lost to the trial and tribulations of the calling my Father has given me."

His father? Who is his father? Is there someone else here? Maggie had to trust her memory, there was nothing to write with. "How did you get here…I mean, why are you living like this? Or do you really have a home somewhere?" The stranger didn't answer. Damn, Maggie thought, she didn't know where to go with this. "What about that little boy? How did you revive him?" Again, moments of silence followed until she turned her eyes skyward.

"Do you remember when, as a young girl, you would wish upon a falling star?" he said. A question so out of context, Maggie had to recollect herself.

"No, no I don't think so. My parents always told me it was a silly thing to do," Maggie responded.

"That boy at the lake did wish upon a star; to be like his father when he grew to manhood. I merely reminded him of his wish, told him a star would have fallen from the sky in vain if he left this world so soon."

Maggie accepted this answer to her question, though she knew it gave no explanation as to how, or even if he did save the boy's life. It was just the way he said it, such finality and conviction! Letting her know there would, or could, not be another answer. Maggie moved closer, her head spinning between confusion and amazement at this individual she was with.

"Where is your father? You mentioned him before: is he nearby?" Maggie asked.

"My Father..." the stranger whispered, "is everywhere."

"Who are you...really?" Maggie whispered back.

Sometimes, in someone's eyes, everything you need to know, or suspect of a person shines luminescently: the mirror of the soul, as is so often said of the eyes. When the stranger turned his head, his eyes coming in sight of Maggie, she gasped at the depth and distinction they revealed. She felt it was her very soul that reflected in his gaze. The vastness of this clear, evening sky was contained in that glance. "My God," she muttered lowly.

"You have what you came for, Margaret," the stranger said, "it is best that you rest now. In the morning you will be home." He raised his hand and gently placed it on the side of Maggie's face, and she relished the softness, assuredness of his touch. It was so relaxing this way, so soothing. She knew she needed sleep and that she would sleep, comfortably and peacefully. Maggie found herself in a dream: she was a child again, outside her parent's home, staring up at a night sky so radiant with stars. Suddenly a flash across the heavens and young Margaret Magdalan closed her eyes and wished with all her might.

When again she awoke Maggie felt everything around her moving. There was noise and confusion, and a low, steady hum, and she again fought for consciousness. She was lying down on her back, looking up at a low, white ceiling that moved when she did. Hovering over her were a man and a woman, on either side. They wore blue outfits which Maggie recognized, and which put a bearing on her surroundings.

"It's alright, ma'am," the woman said, as she adjusted a gauze-wrap around Maggie's head, "You've been in an accident, but you'll be fine. Just a nasty bump. We're taking you to the hospital just to make sure." Slowly, they lifted the gurney she was on and placed her further into a waiting ambulance.

Did she dream all of it? Could the stranger have been only in her mind? She made no effort to speak, just closed her eyes and fell back to sleep as the ambulance that carried her sped down Seven Lakes Parkway, disrupting the serenity of the dawn with its wailing sirens. From atop a nearby hill, the stranger stood in the morning shadows and watched the vehicle disappear.

X

"Honestly, Maggie, how could I run this?" her editor said. David Brantley was one of those men who held onto his boyhood looks making it impossible to guess his age if you didn't know him. At thirty-eight he was young for a chief editor, but his father owning a large part of the newspaper had a lot to do with that. Not that he wasn't good at his job: he was very good. He knew what he was doing and he was always fair.

"Why not, David," Maggie asked, "I know what you're thinking, that it's very speculative, but don't you believe me?" Brantley scanned through the story again. He was one of those types who kept his finger on the page as he read, pointing to each word, sliding quickly through each sentence. A habit he developed to not lose his place during the constant interruptions his position demanded.

"There's no question in my mind, Maggie, that you believe this is what happened to you and that you did meet this guy. It's the best piece I've ever gotten from you, but you yourself admit there's nothing tangible to go on, to prove this fellow is really out there. No photographs, no idea where this cave actually is...jeez, you didn't even get his name! You have no idea how you got back to the car and the emt's said it didn't seem you were moved after you hit your head on the steering wheel. That's where they found you, still in the driver's seat. Maggie, I'm sorry but this story breathes of fiction, of maybe a dream you experienced after you were knocked unconscious. It's dangerously close to a supermarket tabloid piece."

That hurt, Maggie thought, this seemed her one chance to elevate the career she chose and it was slipping away. Normally, she was in control of her emotions but this time she felt the tears running down her face and she couldn't stop them. Brantley looked up from his papers just as the last tear fell, he quickly looked down again as Maggie turned her head away. This story really must mean something to her, he thought. His father would tell him Maggie Magdalan was the newspaper's treasure and it was important to keep her happy. In a quieter and sullen tone David Brantley spoke: "Tell you what, Maggie. I'll run it on a back-page, and only if we use a different byline. If this backfires I don't want to jeopardize your "At Home" series. Don't want the public to know it's the same writer. Is that fair?"

Maggie knew David expected an immediate answer, one that bordered on enthusiasm, but she couldn't help but hesitate with a response that came from resignation. It was better than nothing at all, she supposed. "I...I guess that will be fine, David," and with nothing more to be said she rose from her chair and turned to leave.

"Wait, Maggie," David said, holding up the papers with the story on them, "what header do you want on this article?"

With the door opened and not turning her head back, Maggie answered: "The Messiah of Harriman," and she shut the door behind her.

Brantley ran the story the next day as part of an inside column the newspaper labeled "Local Whimsies". The column would run submitted stories by readers about peculiar events that occurred in and around the Sloatsburg area. Generally, the column's aim was for amusement believing readers never took too seriously the stories that appeared once-a-week in its space. But "The Messiah of Harriman" was different. It was credited to a Judith Cariotta and Brantley believed it would be nothing more than a passing diversion to his readers as they went about their daily lives. He was wrong. He couldn't have known how quickly word-of-mouth had spread throughout the area of the stranger's appearance and the deeds he performed, so when the story came out, again word-of-mouth had everyone run for their copy because everyone knew someone who knew someone who actually saw this stranger perform a miracle. The offices of The Sloatsburg Daily were flooded with calls from those who met the stranger, who grew up with him, were saved by him, but there were those from callers who labeled the paper blasphemous, who screamed into the phone it was the work of Satan to glorify this false prophet. David Brantley felt overwhelmed but he was greatly relieved at least by his decision to keep Maggie's name off of the byline.

XI

"...and finally, on our evening broadcast," said the anchorman on Channel 2's television news out of New York City, "it seems an item published by a local Sloatsburg, New York newspaper ran some weeks ago, about an individual who resides somewhere in the confines of Harriman State Park, has created quite a basket of rumors as to who he actually is. This man was been able to elude public scrutiny, until recently. According to this newspaper article entitled "*The Messiah of Harriman*", this person has not identified himself, many of the locals calling him simply a stranger. There are those in the area - descendants of the Algonquian Indians who have lived in southern New York State for countless generations - who call the stranger '*Gitche Manitou*', the name of an Algonquian deity. According to sources, this man first appeared some months ago when, as told by witnesses, he seemingly brought a boy back to life who, by all purposes, had drowned in Harriman's Lake Tiorati. Since that occurrence, there have been numerous stories of this man's appearing and disappearing while performing... er, 'miracles', if you will. One elderly gentleman lays claim to having his eyesight restored by this stranger's visit. All of the stories we heard about were not verifiable. The article in the paper was written by a Judith Cariotta who states she spent some time with this 'Messiah' in his mountain cave. These aerial shots we are showing you now are of the main artery that cuts through the south end of Harriman Park's Seven Lakes Drive, that originates in the town of Sloatsburg, New York, coming off of State Highway 17. These images were taken Sunday and you can see the volume of vehicles that form a line of cars nearly the entire length of the road's stretch. This road and others in the park have been experiencing a glut of people and traffic since the newspaper article appeared four weeks ago.

"Local officials and park rangers have expressed concern over the volume of visitors, over-taxing the park's security and maintenance. Bear Mountain officials who oversee the park's security have said they don't believe this individual exists. The editor of *The Sloatsburg Daily* has been criticized severely for what many have called the antics of a supermarket tabloid. Well..." the anchorman closed sarcastically, "if this man is found, I'm sure Big Foot will be right behind him!"

XII

Locked within, and not without,
forever raising within me as a burning
seed. I see, I learn, I know, I desire...

I need Him

A light, misty rain covers the land in these pre-dawn hours. Normally, the first glimmer of morning hues could be seen faint over the eastern mountain tops of Harriman, but the overcast sky has delayed this morning's arrival. The stranger has been kneeling for hours in prayer at this vantage point over Lake Welch. He is drenched and shivering but the vigil must continue for it is time to seek the answers he needs from the Father. His face turns skyward, towards the cloudy skies which are already beginning to disperse. From where he is he can see Seven Lakes Drive and already the flow of humanity is arriving, though fewer people have come these last few days. Still, those who seek the truth are here every morning and linger until the rangers ask them to move as the day's light disappears. They have waited patiently, and hopefully, they will not wait much longer.

There were times these last few weeks when some came close to discovering him. Those ambitious souls who wandered far from the roads, but no one knows this land like him, and it was easy to blend into the forest's cover when he needed to. No longer...the hiding is over. He kneels again before his God and asks the same questions, hoping that what he feels in his heart are the answers. Soon, the stranger will be among them and the journey will be near its end.

XIII

Halfway into the Sloatsburg village meeting that included officials from nearby towns, everything seemed to rest on the shoulders of Sloatsburg police chief Dan Hill. Representatives from New York State's Park Rangers and State Police said their piece: they are doing their job, under the circumstances. Controlling and keeping order among the large volume of visitors Harriman has been getting. The curiosity seekers, newspeople among them, were overflowing onto the property of Sloatsburg homeowners and many thought Chief Hill could be doing a better job. He disagreed. Woefully understaffed, his small force was at the point of exhaustion, answering every disturbance and complaint possible. Chief Hill reminded the meeting he didn't write the cockamamie newspaper article and the Sloatsburg Daily should be held accountable to some degree for all this hoopla.

"Just a moment, chief," David Brantley spoke up, standing to interrupt the chief's dialog, "if I might have a few words?" Sloatsburg's mayor Edward Nadler slammed his gavel down.

"Mister Brantley, the proper procedure is..."

"It's fine with me, Ed." Chief Hill interrupted. 'Mr Brantley can have the floor."

David Brantley moved from this aisle seat to the floor area in front of the mayor's podium. "Gentlemen," he began, "for those who don't know me, my name is David Brantley, editor of the Sloatsburg Daily, the newspaper that ran the story about this individual they've been calling the Messiah of Harriman. To begin with, I would like to dispel these accusations of 'rag' journalism we have been accosted with. The piece was submitted by a reader and placed into a section of our newspaper that runs stories of whimsy and fantasy. Henceforth, our decision to print this story was based on sound trust and principles that we have in our readers to understand that distinction. We never anticipated the catalyst it would produce, the occurrences of the last few weeks. During this time we have cooperated with local authorities, investigating every rumor, or purported sighting of this individual. We, like all of you, are hoping to confirm or dispel his existence. We have also informed the public, through our newspaper, of all steps we have taken."

"And what have you found so far?" asked Mayor Nadler.

Brantley turned towards the seats behind him in the small municipal court room of Sloatsurg: "Not a thing, Mr Mayor, but at this point it means very little. Harriman is a very large and complex area and anyone with a good knowledge of the park would be capable of evading detection even from an intensive search. We just don't believe he can hide forever."

Chief Hill smiled a sly grin to no one but himself after Brantley sat down. How convenient, he thought, for Brantley's newspaper to be so generous in assisting in locating this guy, which at the same time shouldn't hurt his paper sales. The chief, like so many others, found it a growing obsession to locate this person. Even on his time off he found himself hiking through Harimann, investigating every square mile he was able to cover in the light of day, and sometimes into early evening. All he found were other's seeking the same 'prize', he called it, but he thought his search different. This quest was a duty, to his job and the people he served. There was something about this mysterious figure that drove him to seek his audience, that increased his determination with every day he came up empty. Chief Hill felt he was seeking an answer to a question he had never asked.

The mayor's gavel coming down to adjourn the meeting startled the chief from his daydream. "Excuse me, chief," he heard from behind him. He turned to see David Brantley approaching. "Chief, do you have a moment?" Chief Hill had no time for a yes or no response before Brantley continued: "Any indication or clues as to who this person is or where he could be hiding?"

"None," Chief Hill responded, "to tell you the truth , Brantley, I can't even tell you why we're looking for the guy? If anything's wrong here your rag's to blame, not some poor schmuck hiding in the hills somewhere." Brantley looked uncomfortable after the chief's tirade. "Look, Brantley, our department's under a lot of pressure to find him. Even the governor's office wants this thing resolved because of the amount of publicity it's getting. But if we find him, then what? He didn't write the article and the only charge would be vagrancy if he's living in the park. Seems an awful lot is being done to find one vagrant."

XIV

Maggie Magdalan was staying secluded. With the furor of the events since her The Messiah of Harriman story appeared, even though she used a pseudo name for the byline, she believed there were stares from her colleagues and even strangers, each one suspecting it was she who caused all of this. She continued her At Home with Maggie column but her ambition and determination to learn the truth of who this stranger is became a compulsion. With what little she had, she began with an assumption, an assumption that only she could have since she was the sole person on this earth who spent time with the stranger. He appeared to be, roughly, about twenty-five to thirty years of age. Using this information, she began an exhaustive search through her newspaper's archives. Hour upon hour behind the microfiche machine, reading birth notices, real estate transactions, missing person reports, police logs, reader letters: all from the last thirty years. She examined anything she thought might provide a clue, if the stranger was from this area to begin with. Maggie didn't know what she expected to find since she really didn't know what she was looking for. She had some distant hope that something that appeared in the newspaper in the last thirty years might lend a clue. Her intentions were if she could find nothing in the Sloatsburg Daily then she would visit other newspaper offices in nearby towns, libraries, municipal records. Wasn't this how good reporting was done, she thought? Tirelessly, night after night for weeks on end she scanned the newspaper's past, from thirty years prior. She covered twelve years after only a few weeks and her hope was fading knowing she had so much microfiche yet to examine.

Then it was there.

An article in the newspaper, front page, from eighteen years ago, the disappearance of Thomas O'Malley Jr. The article told of his disappearance during a night his father was out hunting. The boy was only twelve. There was a massive search party put together: dogs, helicopters, citizens who volunteered searched for weeks and weeks but no sign of the boy was ever found. She remembered this event. At the time, Maggie was in her early thirties, just starting the At Home with Maggie column and she remembers the commotion in the news room each day. Thomas O'Malley Sr was a popular cop in Sloatsburg, friends with David Brantley's father and the newspaper used all it had to aid in finding his son. They searched months but with the onset of a severe winter it became a recovery mission. The boy's body was never found. Thomas O'Malley Sr took leave of his patrolman job to search on his own for another six months until he too had to admit that his son being alive was unlikely. Maggie also recalled that his wife passed away a few years later, his 'estranged wife' the obituary read.

Why did this particular report intrigue her? She'd read other missing persons reports in the last few weeks. What was it? She read and re-read the original police report. It said what the boy was wearing, plus he was carrying his Remington rifle and a boy's backpack with a Superman logo…My God, Maggie realized, the pillow in the cave! The one my head was on when I woke up. That HAD to be the backpack, it makes sense now, but why hadn't someone put this together? She pulled out her *The Messiah of Harriman* article: the mention of the makeshift pillow wasn't in there! Either she forgot about it, or it was edited out.

Maggie called David Brantley even though it was nearly midnight. He answered sounding like he obviously was awoken by her call. "David", she yelled excitedly in to the phone, "I think I know who he is. The stranger. You have to come to the office!"

Anger was what most men would have experienced, getting a call this time at night at home over a not-so-dire matter, but David Brantley grew up in a newspaperman's household and he remember his father getting these calls in the middle of the night during the war with Germany. His father's advice was never lose your cool because great stories don't have a nine-to-five schedule. "I'll be there soon" he said into the receiver before hanging it up.

Twenty minutes later, it was only the two of them in the press room of the Sloatsburg Daily. The nighttime cleaning crews had finished up and gone home. Maggie related to Brantley all about her recent discovery, laid out the timeline of Tom O'Malley's son disappearing eighteen years ago and he'd be about thirty now and that this stranger looks to be about that age. "Do you realize how absurd this sounds, Maggie?" Brantley questioned her, "I remember that boy's disappearance. Every resource possible was used to locate him, never found a trace. Even if he stayed alive for a month or two, out of sight, he would never have survived that harsh winter. Not counting all the years and winters since. It's just not feasible."

"Look," Maggie replied, "we've got nothing else to go on. Not being probable doesn't mean it's impossible. This guy shows up, seemingly out of nowhere and knows the area well enough to fade out of sight after each appearance. It would take time, a lot of time to learn the park's terrain to that extent. Consider the crowds this news brought, all of these religious flakes, people just curious, all the attention he's getting…thousands of people covering every square foot of Harriman and still nothing of the man or where he could be. Now the crowds are thinning out, their interest has peaked. He might be preparing to show himself again believing there's less chance of getting caught."

Brantley pondered her words, scanning over her notes and maps of Harriman State Park spread out before him on the table. The map was highlighted in yellow the areas where the stranger was reported. The police had tried to triangulate the points on the map, hoping to condense the region he might be hiding it, but it was no use. The area was too large, too many possible hiding spots. Plus the fact it was a half-hearted search since there wasn't a particular charge to hit him with, other than vagrancy. Unlawful assembly if he appeared before a crowd, but that didn't happen. "Let's talk to Chief Hill in the morning, but for now, go home and get some sleep. God knows you'll need it tomorrow. You realize we'll have to let him know it was you who wrote the article."

XV

Chief Hill laughed. "You're kidding, right? Tom O'Malley's boy? Damn, Brantley, you'll come up with anything to sell papers."

"Chief, my reaction was the same as yours when I first heard this theory, but I've know Maggie for a good many years. My father trusted her, I trust her. All we're asking is for you to consider the possibility."

"Of what?" Chief Hill interrupted, "that a twelve-year old boy who disappeared nearly twenty years ago might still be alive and masquerading in Harriman State Park as a what? a righteous do-gooder with magical powers? Chrissakes, you two... don't know if I should be angry or amused!" By this time, the chief's elevated voice had drawn the attention of patrolmen and detectives who were working at desks outside of his office. They could see their boss getting flustered and anxious, his movements becoming more animated. "Out, now!" Chief Hill yelled, "and don't waste my time with this crap."

Maggie and David Brantley had no choice, the chief could not be reasoned with just now. Walking ahead of Chief Hill they exited his glass-enclosed office when they stopped, their attention drawn to the door at the headquarters front. Everyone in the room stopped what they were doing, staring at the figure who stood before them all. He was wearing a hooded sweatshirt pulled up over his head, his long hair sticking out of it by his neck. He was wearing jeans and sandals and though he was ragged in appearance and in need of a bath, he presented an image of serenity, of peace.

"I am he" was all he said.

XVI

I am but a part, if only
to surrender. I have already
lived far too long.

I Love Him

Cautiously, he listened, easily able to distinguish the sounds of the forest from the sounds of men. He heard the shouting, but just as easily heard the whispering. Though low and barely audible, nevertheless it was there, the whispers of those creeping through the pine forest, stealing over the forest floor, trying so hard to be careful, quiet, not wanting to make even the smallest twig snap. It didn't matter: he could hear them, hear their very thoughts. He knew what they wanted of this Son of Man, the questions, the requests, the pleas. For the first time he was frightened. How easy it would be to hide, but not now. Hiding was no longer in the plans. So, he sat quietly, still, like the mighty oak when there is no wind to move it. It was time to put his faith in the hands of these Judas Escariots! When the last whispering voice moved on, he rose from where he was and began another journey, down Seven Lakes Drive, into the town of Sloatsburg and up the steps of the Sloatsburg police department.

The slight furor in the squad room over the stranger's appearance slowly escalated to a somewhat chaotic situation. While some of the men there stood in disbelief that this surly individual was the one causing all the mayhem, others found his appearance humorous, snickering or even laughing out loud at the "nutcase" or "beatnik" who stood in their doorway. Until he looked at them. His eyes were a penetrating, even disturbing blue, seeming capable of seeing into your very soul, discovering your darkest secrets, and even those hard-core men, the ones who'd seen the horrors of war and man's inhumanity to man, became unsettled when his eyes met theirs.

Chief Hill escorted the stranger into his office where Maggie and David Brantley followed him back in, he led him to a seat opposite his desk. "Hello, Maggie. It is good to see you again," he said, confirming to the two other men in the office the validity of Maggie's story of having met this man previously.

Maggie hesitated in her reply, letting this moment take effect for what was happening: "Hello, sir," she responded somewhat lamely. She knew his greeting deserved a better, more welcoming salutation but her mind was at a blank as to what would be sufficient.

Chief Hill spoke next: "I'm glad you came in, sir. We've been looking for you for some time now. There are questions we have that need answers. To begin with, can you tell us your name?"

There followed an awkward moment of silence, the stranger looking out the window onto the streets of Sloatsburg. "I was among you more than once," he began, "my actions were answers to the questions being put before me then. Questions you could never understand but that I answered in the way my Father requested."

Oh boy, Chief Hill thought, we've got a live one here. "What is your name? Do you have any identification with you?"

"Whatever I was called in your world has long since cease to matter. I answer to friend, messenger, brother…"

"Enough," Chief Hill interrupted, "either give us a name, tell us where you're from or we'll be holding you for twenty-four hours while we send out your picture to other towns and counties checking for any outstanding warrants for someone matching your description. Vagrancy, unlawful assembly, disturbing the peace…any number of laws I can charge you with. Do you understand?"

The stranger continued his gaze out the windows. In his head he could hear the voice of angels, crying again for him and what they knew was his destiny. He didn't respond to Chief Hill's tirade, turning his head to look at Maggie. "Are you feeling better today, Margaret? I was concerned about that bump on your head."

"Sonnofabich!" Chief Hill screamed, "I haven't got any time for this bullshit! I think…"

"Just a moment," David Brantley interrupted, deciding to address the elephant in the room. "Sir," he began," do you know who Thomas O'Malley is?" With that, he pulled the photos of Thomas O'Malley Jr from the folder he was carrying and laid them before the stranger, fanning them out on the desk. The stranger looked down at each one, studying each picture carefully. Brantley looked from the photos to the man in the chair before him, searching for any similarity in appearance. It was impossible to discern due to the age difference and with the stranger so disheveled and having a beard. The photos of Thomas O'Malley Jr were black and white making it impossible to tell the color of his eyes, but Brantley also had a copy of the original newspaper article of his disappearance and it mentioned the boy's eyes were blue. He leaned over to Maggie and pointed this out in silence. He took Chief Hill aside, told him what he thought about getting Tom O'Malley in here to meet the stranger. He would know if this was indeed his own son.

"And when he discovers it isn't?" the chief asked, "Then we're dragging up a painful memory for Tom based on a far-fetched speculation? How fair would that be?"

"Chief," David Brantley answered, "we've got nothing else."

XVII

Tom O'Malley was on his way back from a trip to Albany, NY having delivered a woman who was wanted by state authorities on forgery charges when he received a call from police dispatch. "Tom," the dispatcher said, knowing O'Malley from having worked several years on the force, "the chief wants to see you as soon as you get back."

"Do you know what this is about?" O'Malley asked.

"No idea, Tom, but he stressed it was important." the dispatcher replied.

"Ten-four. My eta is approximately twenty minutes."

In the meantime, Chief Hill moved the stranger into a holding cell in the station basement. He advised his officers and detectives to stay clear, not to speak to him on any matter. There was a small crowd and a contingency of local reporters gathered in the station lobby that caught wind of the stranger's incarceration, wanting to catch a glimpse of the man who supposedly performed miracles in Harriman State Park over the last few months, many of them conjured up by an imaginative, or hopeful, public. Chief Hill had the lobby and the street cleared, telling everyone he wasn't the man they were looking for, it was just someone brought in on a trespassing violation. Lying was not his forte, despite being a cop for so many years, but he didn't need the aggravation of a turbid afternoon being more confusing than it already was. The stranger offered no resistance, still offered no name or address and Chief Hill had no recourse except to photograph him and send his description and fingerprints out on the wire. He could hold him for twenty-four hours and if nothing comes back he'd gladly let him go, but maybe deliver him to the state hospital in Albany. The head-shrinkers up there would know what to do with him.

When Tom O'Malley walked into Chief Hill's office, the chief could hardly get himself to look him in the eyes when he greeted him. Maggie and David Brantley had already left; they still had a newspaper to put out. Chief Hill implored them to hold off on any story that says they were holding the man everyone was looking for until they got some answers. They reluctantly agreed but only when promised they would be the first to be made aware of any new developments.

"Danny, what's this about?" Tom O'Malley inquired. "What's so urgent?"

"Tom, I have a story to tell you and I need you to have an open mind when I do. God knows I haven't been able to but this is an angle we have to explore. You're aware we have the guy from the park who's been raising the dead, or whatever, right?

"Yeah, heard it over the radio on my ride down. What's that got to do with me?"

With that, Chief Dan Hill explained the entire matter, word-for-word to Tom O'Malley, detailing the similarities between the stranger and his boy who went missing so many years ago, the theory explored by Maggie Magdalan and David Brantley. He told Tom about the backpack with the Superman logo on it and how Maggie says she saw it that night in a cave where the guy was living, supposedly. Chief Hill made it clear it he didn't ascribe to the theory, thought it was preposterous, but that they've tried everything else to identify the guy since he won't tell us who he is or where's he's from, so every possibility, no matter how far-fetched, needs to be eliminated.

"Personally, I think he's a nut-case, Tom. He needs to be in a hospital and will be if we don't get any word on…"

"Let me see him," Tom O'Malley interrupted. During Chief Hill's dissertation, O'Malley relived the night of Tommy Jr's disappearance, the months and months of searching without finding so much of even a trace of the boy. Dan was there, he remembers what he was going through, he knows there was never any closure. The probability of this stranger being his lost son was low, off the charts, but the chance of this man being part of the closure Tom O'Malley never found was more of a possibility once this door was closed and Thomas Jr pushed even more into the background of forever lost.

"Tom, are you sure? Do you want me to go downstairs with you?"

"No, Dan," Tom O'Malley replied, "I need to do this alone. Need to speak to him without anyone there. You understand, right?"

There was no need to answer yes or no from Chief Hill. "Let me know what I can do," was all he said as Tom O'Malley left his office and headed for the holding cell where the stranger was being held.

In the confines and quiet of the Sloatsburg Police holding cell, the stranger kneeled in prayer in the dimly lit cell of iron bars and cinder block walls. The air was damp and cool and he welcomed the solitude as he offered his soul to the Heavens in silent repose. He never lifted his head when he heard the door at the top of the stairs open and close, nor did he look up when the sound of boots could be heard descending the basement stairs. Tom O'Malley approached the cell tentatively, almost regretting his decision of bothering to check this guy out when he discovered him kneeling on the floor by the cot. My boy wasn't religious, he thought, we weren't church people, so even more reason to believe this can't possibly be him. When Tom O'Malley stood at the cell door, the stranger moved from his kneeling position to sitting on the edge of the cot as he looked into the eyes of the detective. Nothing was exchanged between them for a few moments, O'Malley scanned the man's features for anything recognizable, anything that he might be able to say positively yes, this could be my boy. After what seemed like interminable silence, Detective Thomas O'Malley spoke: "Tommy?" was the only word he uttered in a moment of distant hope and nearly a lifetime of despair.

"It is your boy you seek?" the stranger asked.

"Yes, but how did you know I asked about my boy?" O'Malley replied. With that response the slimmest of possibilities existed that this was Thomas Jr slipped away.

"There is much I know. You never found your boy, did you? Missing all these years, you never found him yet never gave up hope, never stopped praying for his return. People don't know you as one who is close to God, yet you turned to Him time and again for these answers. Am I right?"

"Right about what? Praying for my son to come home? Who wouldn't, no matter if they believe in Heaven and Hell or not? How do you know any of this, or anything about me? Did you know Tommy? You look about the age he'd be now. If he's alive somewhere, you need to take me to him. It's all I ever want in this life. Maggie saw the backpack in the cave…"

"I can tell you where to find him," the stranger interrupted.

XVIII

The stranger's geographic knowledge of Harriman State Park was beyond anything Tom O'Malley expected. He outlined where the cave was that Maggie Magdalan described, through a series of roads, turns and paths explained in minute detail while O'Malley wrote everything down. When it was over, he held his excitement, his wonder in check. Why did he need to find the cave? The Magdalan woman never mentioned anyone else there besides this guy. "I can't take you with me," he explained, "you need to stay here until we hear back from our wires about who you might be."

"It is better you do this yourself," the stranger said, "what you find is for your eyes only." And with that, Tom O'Malley locked the door behind him. He did not look back as he ascended the stairs back to the squad room. If he did he would have seen the smile on the stranger's face.

"It's not him," O'Malley told Chief Hill. "I never believed there was a chance anyway."

"Alright, Tom. I appreciate your coming down and sorry to bring up old wounds. We'll just wait to hear if there's any record on the guy."

"You got it, Danny," O'Malley responded and left the station. Using the stranger's directions, he drove down Seven Lakes Drive to the first circle, halfway around the roundabout he continued straight onto Seven Lakes Parkway until he came to Lake Shanatati. There was a trail on the north side of the lake, just where the stranger said it was, that ascended slightly upwards into a part of the forest where the trail wasn't visible at all from below. Where the trail began a left turn and downwards descent, there was another narrower trail that climbed up into a series of rocky crags It was here the O'Malley was to locate the boulder that pointed north, the cave was at its foot. It wasn't hard to find the boulder he needed and sure enough, there was a large cave opening at its base. That it had been occupied was obvious, O'Malley noticed the same items that Maggie described that she saw there. In particular, he found the backpack, or the remnants of one, with the Superman logo barely discernible. It was his heart beating hard and rapidly that caused him to stop for a moment and gather himself. There was no one else in the cave, he yelled out for his son. "Tommy", echoed through the crags and forest below. "Son, can you hear me? Are you here?" O'Malley, in desperation and hope, yelled louder with each bellow. He left the cave and searched the area as thoroughly as one man alone could, returning to the cave in between each excursion in case his boy returned.

As dusk approached, he returned again to the cave after another exhausting search through the forest and lake area below.

In the corner of the cave were three stones, placed carefully at the foot of a small mound, flat on the ground touching each other. Why he hadn't noticed them before he couldn't understand but they drew him to where they lay as if he was being pulled. The low mound was maybe four feet in length, and even though it had been carefully maintained he could see it had been there quite some time. O'Malley fell to his knees and began digging with his hands, then with one of the flat stones. He dug at a furious pace, a man possessed with a task, oblivious to the world around him. A few feet down he came across what he feared he might find: it was a small, skeletal hand. He stopped digging and the tears flowed, there was no point in going on because O'Malley knew what was there. He placed a call to his dispatcher, described his location and waited, sitting on the edge of the cave mouth as it grew dark. Through misty eyes he saw the full night sky coming into view. "I'm sorry, Mary." he whispered to no one but himself and a shooting star blazed across his vision cutting through the black of night.

In the shallow grave they found the remains of a young child, most of the torso wrapped in the material from a small tent. With the remains were remnants of clothing that hadn't completely disintegrated and material that was possibly used in raingear. But the defining item was the old Remington rifle buried alongside the body. It proved to everyone that Thomas O'Malley Jr was the one buried in that cave. With nothing else to go on the cause of death was impossible to determine, there were no fractures on any bones. Thomas O'Malley was disinterred and given a proper burial in the O'Malley family plot, next to his mother Mary.

With no cause to hold him the stranger was released after nothing came back indicating he was wanted anywhere else. He walked out of the station before Tom O'Malley returned and told Chief Hill how he came across the location where Thomas Jr was buried. "I wish I'd known," the chief told O'Malley, "would have had a reason to hold him."

"For what?" O'Malley replied, the coroner said my boy was buried there for at least the eighteen years he was missing, and the guy you had couldn't have been any older than Tommy would have been. I can't explain his living in that cave where Tommy was buried but it's a sure bet he didn't have a hand in it. Wouldda been too young."

"Just the same, he might have known something. I've got cops out looking for him again and as before he seems to have fallen off the face of the earth. If we find him I still want him to answer why he knew what he knew."

Maggie was given the task to write the story for the *Sloatsburg Daily* by her editor David Brantley. She detailed from beginning to end the saga of the stranger that once roamed Harriman State Park and how he revealed the information that allowed the police to discover Thomas O'Malley Jr's grave. It was picked up by the New York Times and soon gained national recognition. The Times gave it the title of Maggie's original story, "*The Messiah of Harriman.*"

XIX

"He's walking so near by,
I can almost hear his breathing.
His steps I sense at night when it appears
that I am sleeping.
Let Him come! Let Him come! For soon
I must be leaving…"

He could see Bear Mountain Bridge in the distance behind him. With his task completed he journeyed north, intent to wander until the Father told him here was his next destination. Coming upon a small stream, he knelt for a drink when the mists appeared on the water and he could distinguish the angels, dancing in glee because he walked with them again and the danger of man was once more not there.

About the Author

RjCook is the writer of the monthly column, *The Life Around Me* that appears in the online web magazine **hREALITY Land** (www.hrland.net). He is also the chief administrator for hRL who, along with his partner, Glenn Maida, have produced an online monthly magazine since 2011.

He currently resides in New Jersey with his wife Patricia and for the most part was born and raised there. There were brief residences in Vermont and California that influenced his writing to a great extent.

Besides being a writer, RjCook has a background in proofreading, editing and telecommunications, as well as being an accomplished musician. In his lifetime he has worked as a real estate agent, a wedding photographer, a truck driver, painted curbs, worked as a garbage collector and a pharmacy technician before settling down and eventually retiring from a telecommunications firm.

"Whatever life offers is an experience essential for a writer to shape and mold into expression that a reader can relate to".

Lightning Source UK Ltd.
Milton Keynes UK
UKHW031051240221
379286UK00009BA/468/J